In space, whoever controls the flow controls everything.

PLUMBING SPACE

The Plumber's War

PLUMBING SPACE

The Plumber's War

By

TOM SHEPPARD

Plumbing Space™ • Book One
A Plus Results, LLC
Nevada, USA

www.AccessPlumbingSpace.com

This book was written by the author, with the assistance of artificial intelligence tools used for research, editorial support, and creative exploration.
All artwork in this book was created by the author using AI-assisted tools under the author's creative direction. Copyright is claimed in all artwork as original works of authorship created with AI-assisted processes.

Publisher: A Plus Results, LLC
Nevada, USA
aplusresults.biz
For permissions: permissions@aplusresults.biz
ISBNs
Paperback: 978-1-967548-09-5
eBook: 978-1-967548-07-1
Edition: First Edition

Cover design: Thomas K Sheppard
Interior design: Thomas K Sheppard
Editing: ChatGPT
Printed in the United States of America

Dedication

In his book, *On Writing: A Memoir of the Craft,* Stephen King says, "Remember that 'plumber in space' is not such a bad setup for a story."

Challenge offered.

Challenge accepted.

This one's for you Stephen King.

Contents

Act I A Plumber Out of Water

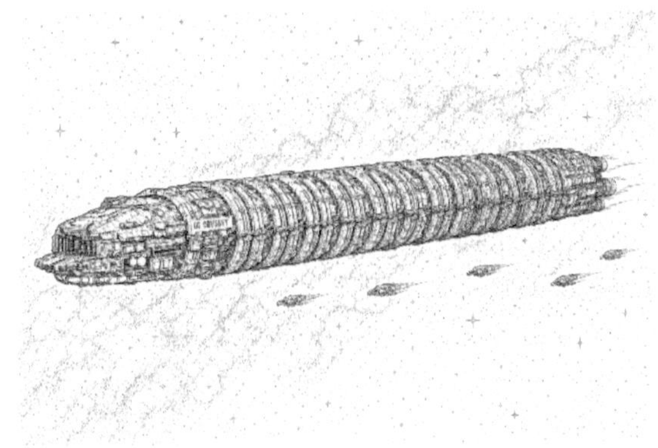

Figure 1 Knuckles

1. The Leak You Don't See

At first, the Odyssey looked like just another smudge, a grain of light swallowed by black. Then it swam into focus: a skyscraper on its side, two kilometers of steel and secrets glinting under a thin wash of distant sunlight. Up close, the Odyssey wasn't smooth at all. The cylindrical hull wore a skin of flat, diamond plates set on shallow angles, a tessellated armor that turned sunlight into hard, crawling flashes—no broad target anywhere, only knife-edges and near-miss planes. When a micro-meteor kissed the shroud, the first plate would take the hit and throw the plume sideways into the dark void behind it; the inner hull, deeper and dull, kept its secrets. Chevron seams marched in mirrored bands from nose to tail, herringboned over the fixed ring frames and pinched tight around the sensor blisters that caught the sun like rivets on a set of brass knuckles. The specs said those were rail guns designed to break up inbound meteorites that might threaten the ship. The crew dubbed the big tube with blunt ends 'the cigar.' Johnny disagreed. 'Knuckles,'[1] seemed a better fit. Like brass knuckles, it looked like Odyssey could deliver a hefty punch.

Cassandra was no dinghy. With a beam of twenty-five feet and a total length of one hundred and fifty feet it impressed him. Johnny first saw her hanging in the void above the moon, looking like a steel coffin with engines, no heat shields, no wings, never feeling atmosphere beneath her hull; a machine designed for the void. Back on Earth, the mob liked Cadillacs with chrome and leather. Cassandra was more like a crew car: plain, boxy, functional. But she could haul men and cargo across ninety million miles without breaking a sweat, and that was all that mattered. Sliding toward the Odyssey, Cassandra felt like a rowboat nosing up against a battleship. The closer they came, the more Odyssey dwarfed them.

Pietro Giovanni "Johnny" Alliata[2] squinted through the thick panes of the Cassandra's viewport into the star-specked

---

[1] See World File: WF-U-003 Odyssey, Access: Union

[2] See Black File: BF-U-006 Blood and Ice Personnel file: Johnny A Access: Union

dark. His identity card, hanging from the left front pocket of his shirt read, "John Andretti."

Johnny, 'The Plumber,' hit man extraordinaire, master of disguise, killer for hire on three continents, had become, at least on paper, John Andretti, Master Plumber, Miami Local 523. 'Giovanni' belonged to Florida, Sicily, and blood debts.

The picture on the laminated card matched his face. Broad forehead, almost square face. Slightly swarthy skin. No beard or mustache. Thick dark hair, graying at the temples. Dark eyes that seemed to soak in everything and give away nothing. Slightly below average height. Trim but not overtly muscular. Otherwise, his image, his bearing, the man, appeared unremarkable.

Johnny chuckled, but it was a dry sound. A plumber in space. That was the gag. Uncle Petie had sold it like a vacation: a no-work union contract, hazard pay kicker, free room and board. A place to lay low while the Gambinos cooled off about Cousin 'Vinnie' Vincenzo's fatal accident in Vegas.[3] Johnny heard it like a one-way ticket to the far side of nowhere.

'Vacation' meant he needed to catch a quick flight out with an indefinite return ticket. 'New start' meant 'don't come back.' In Johnny's mind the jury was still out which this

[3] See BF-U-000 Pipes in the Casino — Johnny A background. Access Union.

was. The difference would be if someone showed up to punch his ticket.

"Read your science books," Petie had said. "Kick back. Safer than WitSec with Marshalls."

Johnny smiled sardonically. "Safer than Witsec? That's not saying much to a man of my talents Petie."

"Poor choice of words," he admitted with a laugh.

Only now, with the Odyssey looming over him, Johnny saw the joke's punchline. This wasn't a pleasure cruise. This was a fortress. A city in the void, stitched together by the cheapest bidder, every mile of it humming with pipes, valves, pumps, and recyclers.

Water. In space, water was worth more than blood. According to all the textbooks and science journals, humanity's insatiable and incessant need for water was the single greatest limit on space travel. It was keeping humanity tethered to the Earth.

Johnny's job was to keep it flowing in space. The Earth was literally covered in water, three quarters of its surface. But, the spaces between the planets was a desert with no hidden wells, ponds, lakes, oasis, or rivers to tap.

The truth hit him harder than any slug thrower: this wasn't a cover job, or a vacation. *This is exile, with a better view.*

If exile was just the bait before the switch to execution, there was nowhere to run, or hide.

2. The Bella Vista

Johnny remembered the night Petie put it to him.

The private dining room at the back of the Bella Vista wasn't a place for the faint of heart, or cops. The room wore its wood paneling like a confession booth; priests, judges, and captains all ate here when they needed a sin to go down easy. Most nights it sat dark and empty, open only for special occasions. Tonight, it was full; the Florida boss celebrating his favorite hit man.

"Johnny my boy!" At forty-two Johnny was far too old to be anyone's 'boy,' but when sixty-seven-year-old Pietro "Petie" Genovese kissed your cheek and called you his boy, you smiled and kissed back.

Petie asked after Johnny's mother, cracked jokes about his father, strolled down the family tree like it was a ledger. Johnny answered every question, absorbed every slight with a smile. In the mob, listening was survival.

Then Petie waved away the food and got serious. "What you did in Vegas, that was great work. Unfortunately, the Gambino family in New York aren't ready to fully appreciate your work. I'm thinking we relocate you someplace cooler. I found you a sweet gig. Safe, steady."

Johnny stiffened. Cooler often meant the grave. But Petie's hands stayed on the table, and Al 'Big Nose'

Campitano, his consigliere, leaned back with a glass of wine in hand instead of steel.

"The Cape," Petie said, grinning. "Plumbers Union's got a contract on that new ship. The Oddity?" Petie turned to Al.

"The Odyssey," Al offered.

Petie's fingers snapped. "That's it. The Odyssey."

Johnny had nearly laughed in his face. "Relocation—to outer space?"

"Perfect cover. Easy money. More miles between you and trouble than Montana and your Uncle Fats could give you."

Johnny smiled, but inside he weighed the odds. Petie was selling it like a vacation. Johnny knew better. No one sent a made man into orbit for laughs. Heat from the Gambinos must be more than Petie had bargained. At least Petie hadn't handed him over to New York. *Outer space or Montana?*" Johnny weighed it, "W*hat a choice. At least there's no cow manure in space.*"

The Odyssey swelling larger in the viewport. Johnny shook his head. *Petie wasn't lying. But he sure as hell hadn't told the whole truth either.*

A shadow drifted across the hull — one of those blisters, close now, bristling with hardware that wasn't in any brochure. Something in Johnny's gut clenched. He tapped the viewport with a knuckle, muttering to himself:

"Every system leaks. The trick is knowing who profits when it does."

The airlock sighed open with a hydraulic hiss, and Johnny, carrying his small bag of personal possessions, stepped from the Cassandra into the belly of the Odyssey.

The first thing he noticed wasn't the scale. It was the smell. Not the sterile tang of scrubbed air, but something faintly metallic, like blood rinsed off cold iron.

The second thing was the sound. Not silence, not exactly. A low thrumming, deep in the bones of the ship, like a pump with just the faintest hitch in its rhythm. Anyone else would dismiss it as background noise. Johnny had spent a lifetime listening for hitches — in engines, in stories, in alibis.

The third was the faces. Crew bustling past barely looked at him, but their eyes slid over his coveralls, clocking "plumber" in an instant. A couple smirked, one even snorted. That was fine. Let them underestimate him. They always did.

Johnny dropped his duffel by his boots and ran a palm across the bulkhead. Cold. Condensation here and there, where it shouldn't be. He frowned. A ship this new shouldn't already be sweating.

"Leaks," he muttered, repeating the mantra that had kept him alive from Miami to Macau. "So, who's profiting from this one." This ship had secrets. And sooner or later, they were going to leak.

Behind him, the hatch to the Cassandra sealed shut with a clang. The little ship was already retracting, leaving him in the care — or custody — of the Odyssey.

Johnny straightened, slung the duffel over his shoulder, and sauntered into the corridor with the loose-limbed walk of a man who didn't care what anyone thought. Inside, his gut tightened. Petie had called this a safe gig. From the smell of blood-metal in the air and the rhythm of the pumps in his bones, Johnny knew one thing for sure, *Odyssey doesn't smell safe.*

3. The First Leak

Johnny muttered to himself, *They sold me a vacation. Instead it was a transfer—off the map.*

Johnny cursed as a globule of water splatted against his cheek, yanking him out of his thoughts. He wiped it with the back of his hand and glared up at the web of pipes crisscrossing the hydroponics bay overhead. White, black, and gray lines snaked above him in bundled runs, vanishing into bulkheads or bending into service trunks like the arteries of a giant steel beast.

The droplet on his cheek had come from somewhere. He traced it back, flashlight beam skipping along the pipes until he found the faint shimmer of condensation. No—not condensation. A pinhole leak.

Droplets floated in lazy arcs, slow-motion bullets in the ship's weak gravity. He tracked them with a professional eye. Not just water wasted, but evidence. Patterns. Pressure cycles that didn't match the schematics he'd memorized. Some were minor—cheap fittings, lowest-bidder welds—but one line pulsed off-rhythm, like a gambler tapping a false tell.

Forty-five minutes later he found the breach — a hairline crack around a cheap fitting. Built by the lowest bidder, same as every mobbed-up construction site he'd ever worked. He patched it in less than a minute, pride tugging a smirk across his lips.

With a hit, no two jobs were the same. This repair? Identical to the last and the one before it. Boring. But he couldn't bring himself to half-ass it. Pride in craft, whether plumbing or killing, was the difference between survival and a dirt nap.

The Odyssey wasn't a million miles from Earth. It was seventy-five million miles away, nearly half an astronomical unit. Half an AU hadn't sounded so bad; until he'd learned an AU was one hundred and forty-nine million miles. That meant this ship was already deeper into space than anything he'd ever imagined.

Outbound on the Cassandra he'd checked the charts a dozen times. If this ship was really about asteroid mining and survey ops, it should have been closer to the Belt, not loitering in this no-man's zone of empty dark between Mars and the Belt. Positioned slightly above the elliptical plane of the solar system.

It didn't add up. Which, in Johnny's experience, usually meant somebody was lying.

Most folks took the easy way on the Cassandra, sleeping through the voyage in drugged bliss. Not Johnny. Too much like climbing into a coffin and trusting someone else to open the box. He'd pushed, wheedled, and finally cut a deal: he'd stand watches, cook, clean, play cards, and in the dead hours bury himself in the Odyssey's schematics. By the time they docked, he knew more about valves and flow regulators than half the kids fresh out of tech school. A plumber by cover, a hitman by craft, and now—damn him—a student of fluids engineering.

Now, weeks aboard, he realized the truth: H_2O was life itself, a controlled commodity. Lose too much, and someone could get spaced. Lose a little, the right way, and someone could get rich.

Black line. Pure, potable water. Pressure's wrong. System read 7.4 bar. His spot gauge showed 7.2, like the feed was being bled off somewhere else and the pumps were compensating. His gut twisted.

Two tenths isn't drift: that's intent. This wasn't about a leak. There was a tap, and a coverup to keep the official readouts green. *One system. Two sets of books. Classic. Who's profiting from this 'leak'?* he wondered.

"Smugglers," he muttered. It fit. Back on Earth, guys stole gasoline with plastic hoses jammed into truck tanks. Here, they were hijacking black-line water, clean H_2O. Easy money if you had a market. Could be a racket.

He opened a report to log the anomaly, then closed it. *The ship keeps one set of books. I keep the other.* He opened a 'black' encrypted ledger of his own and logged the anomaly. He injected the reclaimed globules back into the system. Then, almost as an afterthought, he glanced at the neighboring run of gray pipe.

The gauge there showed a faint dip; lower than spec. He checked the flow chart again. Should've been steady, but it wasn't. He snorted. *Who cares if sewage is running a little light?*

Graywater was shower water and dish suds. *Nobody in their right mind steals dirty bath water.*

White pipes carried sewage, black water from toilets and worse. White pipes show black-water leaks instantly: gross, but it keeps people alive. *You see a white pipe weeping, you run.* Johnny seldom found pressure variances on white pipes. When he did, they always led to leaks and toxic messes.

But the pure water in the black lines, and gray water lines were another story. Lots of oddities in pressure, and more. Something about the lines bugged him. The way the black and gray ran side-by-side for fifty feet, then split in opposite directions, only to converge again a deck lower. He flicked his wrist-comm and pulled the schematic overlay. Sure enough, the junctions didn't match the drawings. Phantom lines; routes that exist in the steel but not on paper. Somebody had rerouted sections and covered their tracks.

He let his gaze slip past the pipes, thinking. Phantom lines, false pressures, mismatched charts. On a union job back home, that would've screamed *fraud.* Somebody double-billing for work never done, or tapping into supply for an off-the-books side hustle. Millions of miles from Earth with nowhere to duck, it could be worse.

Johnny sealed his kit, gave the pipe a last wipe, and muttered, "Every hit leaves a trace. Every leak leaves a trail."

He wasn't sure yet where this one led. But he intended to find out.

On his wrist-comm, he filed the official report—*minor pinhole, section patched, pressures normalized.* Then he opened his private file and added the part that didn't belong in the logs:

Black-line overpressure suggests off-system tap. Gray-line underflow unexplained. Phantom routing at Deck 12-14 junction. Pattern inconsistent with wear. Possible theft or misdirection. Watch Bay 16.

He closed the file, relaxed, and lit an imaginary cigarette he wasn't allowed to smoke. Two sets of books. The official one for the brass. The other, just for him.

And he trusted his books more than theirs.

He muttered under his breath, "Every system leaks. The trick is knowing who profits when it does."

Crawling out from beneath the floor, he shoved his kit through the hole ahead of him. He pulled himself through and onto his feet. Slinging the kit onto his shoulder, he sauntered out of the bay, and muttered to himself with a grin that never reached his eyes: *Every leak's got a reason. Time to find out who's bleeding the Odyssey and who's holding the knife.*

Act II Blood in the Water

Figure 2 Plumber's Closet

4. Plumber's Closet

Don't get caught, was the first rule of murder for hire. Keeping that rule meant each hit was carefully planned and flawlessly executed. Forensic countermeasures to defeat the cops required extraordinary care. His 'science' reading was one reason he was the most successful hit men who had never been caught. No evidence and no witnesses.

Johnny checked the locater. Jack 'Ham' Hamilton, the only other plumber on board, was in their shared 'office,' deep in the bowels of the ship. Johnny rode the service lift down to Deck 16 with a wrench in his pocket and a theory in his head.

No way, this water game runs without Ham tapping the line, or looking away. He's leaving witnesses, and he just got caught. It was time for a heart-to-heart with his work buddy. He palmed the hatch and walked into the stink of copper, solvent —and blood.

Training said water was life. Out here, wasting it or stealing it got you fired—and buying your own ride home. Union paper said Johnny wasn't getting fired. Reality said the leaks didn't care.
It turned out there was a lot of plumbing work in space. Two plumbers couldn't keep up. Every fitting looked like the last. Every fix blended into the next. Hits were never like that. Hits were bespoke. The inside of the Plumbers Closet was anything but bespoke.

Standing just inside the doorway, Johnny touched a button on his wrist computer while surveying the scene for a full minute. Then he stepped back out of the office and opened a line to the bridge.

"Skipper, this is Plumber John. We have a problem."

"Somebody stealing water again Mister Andretti?"

"If only sir. I think you better come down here and see for yourself. Oh, and sir, I suggest you bring your XO with you."

The Captain paused at the unusual request. "Alright. Where are you?"

"Plumbers' Closet sir."

"Say again?"

"The plumbing supply closet. Deck 16, 0 Ring. Compartment 438 Q."

"On my way."

Johnny sat down on his vacuum bucket, designed to suck up loose water in low gravity, and prepared to wait. He craved a cigarette, but that would literally set off alarms unless done next to the specified air recyclers.

It took the Captain nearly nine minutes to find him.

Captain William "Wild Bill" Farragut[4] wore the eagles on his collars and the four stripes on his sleeve with justifiable pride. His steel gray hair was the only evidence of his advancing age. His ramrod straight back and glistening ebony skin showed no signs of bowing to Father Time. The pink scar that ran from his scalp, through his left eyebrow, across his cheek and throat to disappear beneath his collar was the only sign of his service in the Pacific War. Space Force doctors had perfectly matched his artificial eye to his surviving natural green one on the right side of his face.

Right behind Captain Farragut was Commander Niels Grigson[5], as Nordic as any Viking ever imagined. Short cropped blond hair capping a head that looked like a chunk of marble atop a six-foot slab of rock, flashing blue eyes,

---

[4] See Black Files: BF-U-005 Blood in the Scuppers. Personnel – W Farragut. Access Union

[5] See Black Files: BF-U-007 Tahiti Fires Niels Grigson. Access Union

broad shoulders and bulging muscles. The Executive Officer was as much a warrior as Farragut, just younger, and less experienced. Having two such warriors in what was supposed to be a peaceful station beyond the orbit of Earth's moon made Johnny wonder on more than one occasion what might be the real purposes of this station.

"What's this about Mister Andretti? It's pretty extraordinary for a Captain to be summoned by a civilian plumber."

"This is killer, Skipper. But, I won't say you're gonna love it." Johnny didn't get up. He waved a hand at the closed door of the plumber's closet. "See for yourself."

Farragut scowled at Johnny, disliking the lack of military discipline inherent in a civilian who had never been in uniform. He didn't understand why the entire crew weren't military. Forcing a smile, he pulled the door open. He didn't have to step inside. He had seen and smelled death often enough to recognize it immediately. He shut the door and stepped back. The XO stuck his head through the door and then back out again just as quickly.

"Who is it?" Grigson, the Executive Officer asked.

"Since he's wearing plumber's togs, and it isn't me, I'd say it's Ham."

From the moment he'd seen that ruined face and the plumber's togs, one thought stuck: someone had punched Ham's ticket instead of his. *For now.*

5. Thirty Minutes Dead

“Jack Hamilton, sir. The Journeyman plumber. Can't tell from the face sir. It’s been beaten into a bloody stew.” Grigson offered.

“How did it happen?” Farragut’s voice was flat. Devoid of the horror or revulsion that typically rang through the voice of anyone who hadn’t already seen death up close and personal.

Johnny stifled a chuckle, seeing that Grigson had already answered that question before it was asked. "The short answer is, I don’t know. It looks like it may have happened sometime during the last half hour. Doc may be able to tell you better on that. The longer answer is that it wasn't an accident."

“He was murdered?” Grigson challenged.

Johnny blinked and his assessment of Grigson’s intelligence dropped a notch. "Unless he knocked himself out and then repeatedly bashed his face against a pipe wrench until his face looks more like beef tartar than a face, then yes Grigson, he was definitely murdered."

“You said, half an hour. What makes you think he was killed so recently?” Grigson growled, his eyes flashing suspiciously at Johnny.

Unperturbed Johnny answered. "Couple of things. First, I just finished a repair job which started about fifty minutes ago right here when I picked up my repair gear, and Ham wasn't here when I left."

"Assuming you're telling the truth that puts a fifty-minute window on this." Grigson interrupted.

"Second," Johnny went on as though Grigson hadn't spoken, "although I only took a quick look in there before calling the Bridge, the drying of the blood, where it isn't pooled up, looks about right for 30 minutes, give or take five."

"How would a plumber know how long it takes blood to dry?" Grigson growled.

Johnny shrugged. "I read. A lot. Six months ago, the International Journal of Forensic Sciences ran a low-G blood study. Spatter dries fast; pools don't. This looks thirty minutes, tops." Johnny nodded toward the Plumbers Closet, "Personally, I am just glad this section has decent gravity or that crap would be floating through the air ducts by now."

Both officers studied Johnny for a moment, then glanced at each other. A silent message seemed to pass between them, followed by a hint of a shrug from each.

"I'll summon the doctor and post security here," Grigson offered.

Johnny snickered. "Do you want everyone on the ship to know there's been a murder?"

"What do you mean?" Captain Farragut asked.

"How many places on this ship merit posted security watches?"

"Three. The bridge, the reactor room, and the armory," Grigson answered.

"Four." Johnny corrected.

"I think I would know if there were four," Farragut growled.

"I suspect you probably do, but your XO may not."

Farragut's scowl deepened for a second, then retreated to its normal level of intimidation. "Grigson, get the Chief Medical Officer and the Chief Engineer up here. Don't use comms and don't do anything to draw attention. Discretion is the word. Understood? If we can keep this secret a week it will be a miracle, and right now, secrecy is our best tool to catch the killer."

Secrecy was the perfect cover – not to catch the killer, but to give them another clean shot.

This time at him.

6. Blood and Navy Whites

"Discretion. Aye, aye Sir." Grigson snapped a salute, did an about face and in seconds they lost sight of him down the passageway.

A passing crewman raised an eyebrow seeing the Captain staring down at the seated plumber. Farragut forced a smile and a nod at the passing crewman. Farragut's forced smile was more frightening than his scowl and the crew member scurried off faster than a cockroach in the middle of the dance floor at a clogging competition.

"Where can we talk privately?"

"While I would ordinarily be happy to invite us to your office Captain, I think that until this area is properly secured, we shouldn't step away. We can go inside, if you don't touch anything."

"It's okay if you touch things, but not me?"

"My prints and trace evidence are already all over the Plumbers Closet. Yours appearing there would be unusual and cast suspicion for the murder on you." Johnny smiled as he rose and opened the door for Farragut. The space inside the Plumbers Closet was more like a walk-in closet than a coat closet, but with one dead man, blood spatter, and two live men, along with the reek of death, it wasn't where either of them would have preferred to chat.

To John's amazement, Farragut managed to stand in that tight space so rigidly that not a single smudge of blood transferred to his impeccable white uniform.

"I am not a suspect in this murder." Farragut asserted.

Johnny shrugged, "If you say so Skipper."

Farragut ignored John's retort. "Why do you think there are four security watches?" He asked as soon as Johnny shut the door behind them.

"It's not something I think. It's something I know. Bay Sixteen. Off the main hangar. No posted sentries, just two 'busy' crew within arm's reach of steel, always. Two-hour shadows, staggered by one. Mixed genders, 'coincidentally' cross-trained. That's a watch wearing a costume."

"No one is stationed there. You're imagining things."

Johnny shrugged. "My mistake then. But, if I'm right, I expect you might pull it off without the hangar crew catching on if you had say,..." Johnny paused, "Oh crap. The whole hangar crew is part of the security team? All forty-odd of them? Does the Chief of the Deck know too, or is she the only one there in the dark? She'll have your balls for teabags when she finds out you kept her in the dark."

Farragut's scowl evaporated. It was replaced with a new expression, one of respect, tinged with suspicion. "How did you arrive at all this?"

Johnny shrugged. "Hyper-observance is another of my strange hobbies, Skipper. As Ship's Plumber I end up all over this ship at all hours. Lot of access hatches let into the hangar, so I have plenty of occasion to be there at all hours." He looked down at the body of Ham on the deck. "Looks like even more now that the other half of my team just cashed his exit chit."

Farragut studied Johnny more closely than he ever had previously studied any civilian member of his crew. Blessed with perfect recall, he went back over Johnny's file in his mind. Nothing there hinted at him being a spy, or worse, a reporter.

"Whatever you think you have seen outside Bay Sixteen, you will now forget. And, you will never mention it again, to anyone without my express permission."

"And if I do?"

"Then, Pietro Giovanni Andretti, or Johnny A, if you prefer, I will throw you in the brig, find you guilty of murder in a fair trial, sentence you to death, and put you out an airlock. I'll manage most of that after spacing you." Farragut's voice was gravel under a bootheel. "Captains are given wide latitude to run their ships."

"You got that wrong skipper," Johnny smiled tightly in spite of being slightly unnerved by the fact that Farragut knew his full legal, although fake, name. Almost no one living knew it. "I'm no Space Squid you can dress up in a monkey suit and order about. I'm a civilian. A union man. Plumbers and Pipe Fitters Miami Local 523. You flush me, and suddenly toilets stop flushing in every military installation and government office from Miami to Amsterdam. Your name will be on the lips of every contracting officer in the whole

Department of Defense and most of Congress. And nobody'll be talking nice about you."

"Let's make sure it doesn't come to that. Shall we?"

"I'll play nice if you do."

Hearing soft footfalls approaching, everyone on board wore soft-soled shoes, Farragut opened the door of Plumbers Closet and stepped out with Johnny right behind him. The Chief Medical Officer, and the Chief Engineer, the only woman among the top command staff, and the XO arrived. Farragut smiled tightly.

"One moment gentlemen." Farragut touched his wrist communicator which chimed quietly to acknowledge recording mode. "This is Captain William Farragut, of the UER Odyssey, commanding, with Chief Medical Officer Commander Javier Wu, Commander Amina Lafferty[6] the station's Chief Engineer, my Executive Officer Commander Niels Grigson, and John Andretti, Chief Plumber."

The device scanned all those present and, in a quiet voice said, "Identities confirmed."

"I am initiating protocol Tango Alpha Zed Romeo." Farragut smiled to himself at the dark humor. He was about to TAZR John Andretti, and the man would never see it coming. "I am initiating this protocol due to the murder of a civilian crew member and a breach of security protocol Zed Echo Echo." There was a moment of silence. "Authority the Merchant-Specialist Induction Act, Post-War Section 17(c)."

---

[6] See Black Files: BF-U-003 Show Me the Heat Amina Lafferty. Union Access

"Acknowledged." The computer replied in its imperturbable feminine voice.

Johnny looked at the faces around him. Only Farragut seemed to know what he was about. The protocols he mentioned drew only blank stares from the others. Farragut's breathing shifted slightly. He paused the way a sniper does right before he begins to squeeze the trigger. It was a tell. Farragut was about to send rounds downrange, right at Johnny. The hair on the back of Johnny's neck began to stand up.

"Now wait just a minute there Skipper..." Johnny put out a hand toward Farragut, who neither stepped back nor paused.

"By my authority under the Temporary Augmentation Zonal Reserve protocol, I am directly inducting the ship's Master Plumber, John Andretti into the Space Force Reserves at the rank of Ensign and calling him to active duty aboard the UER Odyssey, effective immediately."

"You can't do that." Johnny objected.

The surprise registering on the faces of the others was profound, and unsettling to John.

"Captain, are you sure..." began Grigson.

"Acknowledged. Temporary Augmentation to Zonal Reserves at the rank of Ensign, effective immediately." Besides Farragut, the communicator was the only one not registering surprise. Immediately, the communicators on the wrists of the other four present chimed. Johnny looked at his.

The message was simple. "Welcome to the Space Navy Ensign Andretti."

Suddenly, Johnny realized he'd escaped the Gambinos only to land in a different family with better uniforms and sharper knives.

"Crap in a tuna sandwich." Johnny swore, something he seldom did. "This isn't over skipper."

"Not by a long shot, Ensign Andretti."

7. Cover Maintained

Farragut turned to Commander Wu. "Jax[7], you have a dead man in there. Murdered. Examine the body and tell me what you find out. Nothing is more important for you right now than finding out everything you can about what happened to the civilian plumber, Jack Hamilton. Understood?"

"Yes, sir."

Captain Farragut looked at Wu, still standing there, listening to what was happening. "Now, Commander Wu."

"Yes, sir," Wu snapped a salute and then stepped away to enter the Plumbers Closet, turning his wrist communicator to scanning and recording modes.

"Oh, and Doc," Johnny injected.

Wu paused. "Yes?"

Johnny smiled, "Quarantine Ham. A gut bug. Wet and loud at every opening. Easily transmitted. Nobody crowds a guy with that action."

Wu looked at Farragut, who nodded. "Use that, and work alone. No team."

"Aye Sir."

---

[7] See Black Files: BF-U-004 Chain of Custody Javier Wu. Union Access

"Lafferty," Farragut turned to the Chief Engineer. The only woman on Farragut's command staff, Amina Lafferty cut her teeth on technology as a child when her father, a radio engineer from Ghana taught her to build communications arrays from scrap. What looked like geometric henna tattoos on her knuckles were actually capacitive controls for her wrist pad. Raised in Accra and Dakar, she was fluent in English, Wolof, Arabic, and technical profanity. Her dark skin and even darker hair glistened like she was in full sunlight, instead of the pale wash of light in the guts of the Odyssey.

"Priority One, rig covert security monitoring inside and outside the Plumbers Closet and Ham's quarters. Install coded door locks on both. Give the code only to Ensign Andretti, who will immediately change it and give me the updated code so that only he and I will know the current code. Nothing comes before this. Supervise it closely and personally. Clear?"

"Yes, sir." Lafferty saluted and turned to go.

"Amina," Farragut fired off a last shot at Lafferty, "if anyone asks, tell them we're covertly gathering evidence because we suspect the plumbers are running a black market for water."

"Monitoring a crooked civilian puke. Aye. Aye, sir."

"That's just mean, Skipper. You too, Lafferty. I'm a puke?" Johnny smirked.

"*Crooked civilian* puke," she corrected. "Gotta keep your cover, *Ensign*."

"Gentlemen, one more thing." Farragut's raised voice stopped everyone in their tracks. "We have no civilian or military police on Odyssey. As joint military and civilian vessel under control of the Navy we didn't need one. Security or military police duties are rotational roles. Who among the military or civilian crew knows anything about how to properly, and discreetly, investigate a murder?"

The three in uniform shook their heads. Grigson added a respectful, "No one sir. We don't even have an S2."

Farragut's gaze rested on Johnny. "Well Andretti, until further notice, I hereby appoint you to be Chief Investigator and my S2. To solve this murder, I grant you authority to question any, and all, of this crew as you may need. While you are investigating this murder, you will do so undercover and continue your work as Chief Plumber. You will not reveal your role, or your commission as a Space Force Officer to anyone without my express permission. Is that understood, Ensign Andretti?"

John's mouth opened, ready to tell Farragut to go screw himself. Johnny saw Farragut's breathing pause. In his head he could hear the safety sliding off as Farragut took aim. The warning voice in his head screamed, *Incoming.*

Farragut smiled, a look that reminded Johnny of the face of a lion he had seen, right before it pounced. Johnny felt a cold drop of moisture run down his spine. *Nowhere to hide.*

"Yes, Skipper."

"Excellent." Farragut made a notation on his wrist recorder.

The wrist units chimed in chorus. BREVET: Lt. Commander (Acting), S-2.

Johnny exhaled.

"Piss on my leg and call it rain."

8. Military Intelligence

Plumbers can make it rain like that too. Johnny told himself.

Farragut turned to his senior officers. "Please coordinate all your activities with the XO and cooperate fully with our new S2's investigation," he seemed to take special delight in Johnny's military role, ignoring the uncomfortable feet shuffling of the other officers. "Although I shouldn't need to say it, I will. Everything about this matter is Yankee Zulu Top Secret. Reveal nothing of this to your subordinates. Only encrypted records. XO, please make sure Commander Andretti knows how to make coded recordings."

"Aye sir." Grigson was clearly torn between delight at an opportunity to 'school' Johnny and revulsion at a civilian being instantly given any rank, but especially chagrined that a plumber was suddenly his peer.

"No thanks Grigson." Johnny muttered. "Figured that out while I was still feet down." Feet down referred to being planet-side. Off planet, artificial gravity could point your feet any direction.

Farragut looked pointedly at Johnny.

"What?" Johnny looked blankly at Farragut. "You don't like that I have a way with technology Skipper? It's another of my many hobbies."

"When addressing a superior officer, you should refer to him, or her, as sir." The other officers suppressed their own smiles. They disliked the lax discipline of the civilian crew almost as much as Farragut.

Johnny appeared to carefully consider the admonition. He shook his head. "Nope. Blows my cover."

The steam of Farragut's anger seemed to filter out through his eyes and those of his staff.

"To put a point on it, calling me by any rank would do that too. Outside of our little knitting circle," Johnny smiled and spun a finger to include everyone present. "I'm a civilian *puke*."

"Crooked civilian puke," Lafferty added unhelpfully.

"Exactly," Johnny joyfully agreed.

Farragut's expression was flat, a deadly expression that Johnny knew as intimately as his own. "This isn't over Andretti."

Johnny shook his head. "No Skipper, it sure ain't. I'll solve your murder for you and then you and me are gonna have a real long talk about my career in the Space Force. And, about yours."

Farragut's scarred eyebrow lifted slightly. "Threatening me, Andretti?"

Johnny tilted his head back to meet Farragut's eyes. Neither man blinked. "Skipper, never in my entire life have I threatened anyone. Threats are bluster and bluff. Bluster and bluff are for those who don't have the cards to back their play."

The eyebrow lowered halfway and Farragut nodded slightly. "I see we both play poker the same way."

Johnny smiled, not the usual charming smile he used to make people feel good and look away. Something very different, very dangerous. Farragut saw it for what is was, one lion staring down another above a kill.

Intelligence had just hired a plumber. They had no idea what that really meant.

9. TAZR'd

Grigson, looking on, felt a chill run down his spine. He had seen that smile before—in Tahiti. Marines laughing in a hailstorm of bullets and shrapnel. Men who didn't flinch when the air turned red. He shook it off.

"Captain, if JAG smells this, we'll be testifying in cuffs by lunch time."

"My problem, not yours Niels. Return to the Bridge. I'll be in my Ready Room."

"Call, raise, or fold, Skipper. We're playing the cards we hold." Johnny quipped defiantly. Then, he turned and stepped away with Wu.

Not waiting for a response from Farragut, Johnny guided Wu toward the Plumbers Closet. "Come on Doc. We have a murder scene to take care of."

"First, we need to record the scene, for the record."

"Done," he pointed to his wrist unit. "Encrypted recording of the whole scene." He added for the benefit of the XO. "I wouldn't have been chatting in there with the Skipper if I hadn't already done that."

"Forensics?" Wu queried.

"I finagled myself a pretty fancy wrist communicator. Top of the line. Light spectrums, chemicals, biologicals, toxins, fingerprints, DNA, all covered."

Farragut watched Wu and Johnny walk away. He recalled hiking in Arizona years before when he happened to see a diamond back rattler gliding away from his path, almost invisible against the scenery. Like that rattler, this civilian plumber faded into the scenery one moment, then suddenly appeared, lethal and menacing. *Time to find out more about this plumber,* he thought as he spun on his heel and walked away.

Back in his Ready Room, Farragut pulled up Johnny's file, ordered the computer to initiate some searches, made some notes, and classified the entire thing. With a few keystrokes, he blocked all off-ship communications from Andretti.

He opened a secure channel to Space Command. His boss, Admiral Phoss, came on the screen immediately.

"Bill, what the hell is going on up there? You TAZR'ed a civilian plumber, activated ZEE, and then made that plumber your S2 in under five minutes?"

Captain Farragut smiled, "It seems you know almost as much as me Ben. Oh, and Ben, we need to keep this TAZR and S2 news locked down. Need to know only."

Admiral Benjamin Carter Phoss, one of the youngest flag rank officers in the entire service shook his head in warning. "You know you can't invoke those protocols without me being notified. Come clean. What's up? Is there a problem with the project?"

"Someone's been murdered."

"Murdered? Good God Bill, who would be stupid enough to commit murder on a closed station, millions of miles from any help or chance for escape? And how does that relate to ZEE? Who was killed? Does this touch Bay Sixteen?"[8]

"No sir. The murder may have nothing to do with Bay 16. The man killed was a civilian. A plumber, Jack Hamilton."

"And you TAZR'ed the culprit to be able to court martial him?"

"No sir. I TAZR'ed the Master Plumber because I needed a good detective to find the killer, and he was the closest thing to it."

"Bill, have the gamma rays baked your brain out there? Do you even hear yourself? What you are saying? You drafted a monkey-wrench driving, knuckle dragging, civilian plumber to investigate the murder of another knuckle-dragging civilian plumber." After a moment, "And why did this become a ZEE matter?"

"That knuckle-dragging plumber I drafted, pinged Bay Sixteen."

The Admiral got very still. "He did?"

"Don't worry Ben, he doesn't know what is going on, but he did pick up on the security. None of my command staff has."

"Who talked?"

---

[8] See Black File BF-U-009 The Lieutenant in Bay Sixteen, Access Union

"It doesn't appear that anyone talked. His job puts him all over the ship at all hours. This guy is so observant, he makes my skin crawl. I watched as, in a matter of seconds, he figured out that the whole hangar crew is on the security team and that the only one excluded is the Chief of the Deck."

Phoss went silent for a moment, absorbing Farragut's information. "I'll cover you on the TAZR, S2, ZEE, all of it. But Bill, we need to know more about this overachieving plumber."

Farragut opened his file on Andretti and began dropping queries to the Republic Bureau of Investigation.

"I'm already on it like mud on a grunt." And if he slipped, the brass would hose him off the bulkheads and call it training.

10. Bones and Blood and Water

Inside the Plumber's Closet Wu and Johnny went over the body together.

Commander Javier 'Jax' Wu was an interesting mix of Mexican, Irish, and Taiwanese with a lean swimmer's build in his late thirties. His dark hair, copper skin, and freckles across his nose lent him a boyish look, making him appear younger than his age. A former enlisted Navy Corpsman turned doctor and officer, He knew how to serve as both a doctor and a medical examiner. Autopsies were sometimes required even in combat situations.

"I will have to get his body back to Sick Bay to perform a full autopsy. Not sure how we'll pull that off in secrecy."

"One thing at a time Doc. Give him the good once over here and then we'll worry about transporting, examining, and storing him without letting the cat out of the bag."

"Probable murder weapon." Wu pointed to the pipe wrench lying in a pool of blood on the floor, brain matter smeared all over the head of the wrench. He scanned the wrench image into his wrist unit and punched a couple of buttons. Immediately a green light illuminated its face. "The computer matches the wrench dimensions to Ham's head wounds, and the DNA matches. No prints or DNA on the handle though. It must have been wiped clean before being dropped."

Johnny nodded. Then he pointed to Ham's throat. "What's that?" Wu scanned the area with his wrist unit.

"That is ante-mortem bruising. It looks like his windpipe was crushed by whatever caused it."

Johnny studied the image on Wu's unit. "Analysis? What is the likely cause?"

Wu manipulated the scanner and an answer popped up. "It looks like the knuckles of a human hand." Wu projected a hologram of the image.

"Is this to scale?"

Wu checked the scanner and made an adjustment. The image shrank a little. Johnny held his hand up inside the image. "Right hand." He announced. "Smaller, more delicate than mine. Slightly upward angle, so the killer is likely a bit shorter than Ham."

Johnny stood up straight and stepped back from the scene. He studied the room carefully in silence for a full five minutes. "Here's how I see it. No signs of a struggle. If they had fought, that bucket of acid on the top shelf above you would have fallen to the deck, or onto one of their heads." Johnny pointed to a canister of acid on the top shelf, half its base hanging over the edge.

Wu stood and moved out of the shadow of the container, glancing nervously at it as he moved.

"Killer shocks the throat with the right hand—steals breath—grabs Ham's wrench with the left, one clean strike to the side of the head, then rage turns it to stew."

"Fluorosilicate Corrosive," Wu pointed to the can of acid Johnny had referred to. The label read, *Causes severe burns. Bone demineralization hazard. Calcium antidote gel required in kit.* "Why do you have that here?"

"It cleans bio-contaminants very well." Johnny shrugged. "Ham knew his killer." Johnny continued. "He wasn't on guard and Ham was minutes from death with the first blow. The wrench was a coup de grace, saving him from suffocating."

"But why all this?" Wu waved at the breakage from shoulder to shoulder and up both sides of Ham's neck.

"Looks like a lot of anger." *Or, was it overkill by someone eager to prove themselves to Petie by taking me out?* Johnny's eyes narrowed. "Or maybe something else. Do me a favor Doc, pay special attention to everything below the skin in those areas. What does your scanner say?"

Wu adjusted his scanner and ran it over those areas. His eyes widened at the results. "I must have done this wrong." He recalibrated. "Lamellar folds along the sternocleidomastoid fascia. Biological. Not artifact."

"Gills?" If gill-heads were involved, then maybe this wasn't about me.

Wu nodded slowly. "AguaLibre rumors weren't rumors. The beating makes soup of them, but it doesn't wipe out the underlying tissues. AguaLibre could be motive."

"Implanted gills so they can breathe underwater." Johnny shook his head. "That takes real dedication to dissent."

Wu shook his head. "No surgical scars. These gills look …," he paused, struggling with the implications, "congenital."

"Seems unlikely he was born with 'em," Johnny paused, considering the implications as well. *Not some circus freak either. Alien?*

"I need to tell the Captain."

Johnny nodded. "No one else though. AguaLibre, or something else, this still needs to be kept as secret as his death. Anyone gets too inquisitive about Ham's health, I want to know about it. Understand?"

Wu nodded.

"Doc, is it okay if I touch him now?"

"You didn't before?"

Johnny shook his head,

"Go ahead."

Johnny squatted by Ham's head. There was something shiny cupped in his hand. Johnny pulled a small vial of cloudy water, Ham's blood still smeared across the seal.

"It looks like Ham was running some water tests. You suppose that got him killed?"

"Doubtful Doc. Water's precious here, but a couple cc's of dirty water aren't worth a man's life."

"This is odd." Wu pulled a small spiral notebook out of Ham's back pocket. "That's serious old school. Paper and pencil? Why not use a digi-pad?"

Paper and pencil can't be hacked, Johnny thought. Aloud he said, "Good question Doc." He lifted the pad and pencil out of Wu's hands before the doctor could open it. "I'll take that Doc. Fewer eyes, fewer leaks," he explained, sliding both into his pocket. "Now, let's get Ham out of here without parading a corpse through the ship."

"How?"

"You probably won't like it," Johnny smiled and patted the supply crate the plumbers used as a makeshift table.

Wu scowled, "You're right. But, it might work."

Moments later Ham was vacuum packed in plastic and slid into the crate. Johnny used the plumber's bio-hazard collection equipment to gather up all the blood into another bag which they slid into the crate with Ham. Finally, the two of them cleaned all the bloodied surfaces in the Plumber's Closet. The detritus was also put into another sealed bag and added to the crate. Johnny slapped a bio-hazard warning on the side of the crate.

As they finished the cleanup Wu wiped perspiration from his brow and leaned against a storage rack. Silently, Johnny retrieved two small bottles of chilled water from the samples fridge. Handing one to Wu, he opened the other and drank deeply.

Wu shook his head and then followed Johnny's lead. "Pirated water from the plumber?"

Johnny smiled. "Part of the job requires I routinely collect samples and run tests. Gray, black, and …" he lifted the bottle like it was a champagne flute, "the good stuff."

"You surprise me Mister Andretti…"

"Please Doc, call me Johnny."

Wu nodded. "Jax, or Doc is fine too," he pointed to himself. "You are full of surprises Johnny."

"Like?"

"I don't think I've ever seen a civilian as unruffled by death as you."

"I come from a very tough neighborhood Doc. I was barely out of short pants when I saw my first body." He didn't tell Wu that he didn't just see a body, he did the killing. That was a landslide that shoved the flow of his life in a direction he had planned to avoid.

"Then, you cleaned this space like a professional bio-hazard cleaner."

"Part of my personal ethic, Doc. Leaks make messes. I could just stop the leak and leave the mess for someone else to cleanup, but if they miss something it comes back on me. And on the Odyssey, poor cleanup could cause bigger problems."

He took Wu's empty water bottle. Wiping it down he placed it alongside his in a sterilizer, closed the door, and started the cycle. He turned and pointed to the crate. "We'll pretend this one's an empty I'm dropping off for you." Johnny chuckled.

"What's so funny?"

"On Earth, I've got pals in waste management. Protective of their turf. Turns out, all I had to do to get my own piece of the action was move to the Belt." Johnny made a mental note, *Add a waste-management clause to my union contract. If I'm doing this, I'm getting paid for it.*

The rigid sides of the crate gave no hint of its contents. Wu stepped out of the closet ahead of Johnny. Lafferty was just finishing the security mod in the corridor. Johnny fixed a lifter under the crate and moved it easily through the hatch and into the hallway.

Tilting his head back toward the closet he caught Lafferty's eye. "You can make your mods in there now Lafferty. Don't leave a mess."

An annoyed sneer flashed across her face. "Aye, aye Plumber Andretti."

Johnny's smile ignored Lafferty's venom. "That's Master Plumber if we're tossing around honorifics." He turned to Wu. "Doc, go on ahead. Set up the reception. Make folks busy enough they pay no attention when I bring this in."

Wu nodded and moved away at a sharp clip, Johnny following at a leisurely pace. Not a care in the world.

Med Bay was buzzing and heads down in their work, when Johnny strolled in pushing the bio-hazard container ahead of him.

"Doc?" he called out to Wu, interrupting him from signing off on a subordinate's report.

"In the back Andretti," he snapped. "You'll see the quarantine sign. Going past that could risk you getting as sick as your friend."

"Somehow Doc, I don't think Ham ever wanted to swim in your 'bay.'"

"No one ever does Mister Andretti. Let's make sure no one else goes to swim in Mister Hamilton's end of 'the bay.'"

"No guarantees Doc. When you crack a white pipe like Ham, the stink and spatters hit the most unexpected places." *Gotta make sure anyone else goes swimming in a cesspool with Ham, it isn't me.*

11. Progress

"What progress have you made Andretti?"

Johnny sauntered across Farragut's cabin and sat down on an armchair. Leaving Farragut standing alone behind his personal desk near the outer bulkhead.

Unlike the chairs in the Captain's Ready Room, the ones in his cabin were designed for comfort. The lighting was softer. There was no 'I Love Me' wall full of diplomas, awards and certificates, here or in his Ready Room. A picture of a wife and two sons, both in uniform, sat on his desk. His only other concession to personal decoration was the ceremonial Naval Officer's saber displayed on one wall. *Not a man driven by ego*, Johnny noted to himself.

Johnny cocked his head slightly to one side. "The killer was a pro. The murderer was an amateur."

"A conspiracy?"

"Not two people. Just a killer who was pissed off, panicked, or both. Fast precise kill. No hesitation, professional. Wiped prints off the wrench, otherwise no cleanup, no coverup. An amateur at murder."

Farragut studied Johnny for a moment. Then, he crossed the room to his liquor cabinet. Drawing out a flagon and two glasses he held up the bottle toward Johnny. "Whiskey?" Johnny nodded.

Farragut poured drinks and crossed the room to hand one over and then sat down nearby.

Johnny sipped his drink, feeling the burn as it slid down his throat. He looked deep into the half inch of amber, "I prefer mine on the rocks, but it's only offered neat up here. No water to spare for ice cubes? Not even for the Skipper?"

Farragut didn't rise to the bait. "So, who killed him, and why?"

"Still not clear. It wasn't a spook," Inside his pocket, Johnny fingered the vial of water he had found in Ham's hand. Releasing it, instead he pulled out Ham's notebook and laid it on the table. "Any spy worth their salt wouldn't have left this behind. It was obviously important to Ham. Hell, I'm no spy and it practically screamed at me – I don't belong here!"

"A notebook? That's old school."

"A *coded* notebook."

Farragut reached for it. Johnny slid it away.

"I've got people for that." Farragut extended his hand for the notebook.

"Right now, you've got me for that. Fewer eyes, fewer leaks." Johnny leaned back and took another sip of whiskey.

Farragut's hand dropped. "Ok. Not a spy,"

"Lots of killers to choose from on Odyssey. Marines are trained for it, combat veterans have the experience. Not a black ops type though. They're trained spies too."

"How would you have done this?"

"If I …," Johnny paused, then restarted. "From what I have read, if a pro had done this it would look like an accident. Everyday Ham and I deal with pressurized liquids. A well-aimed pressure leak can cut flesh like a hot knife through butter, but that would mean getting Ham to meet in an out-of-the-way space where one of those tubes is handy. Killing him and then making it look like the hose broke. Done is some dark corner of the ship, it might have been hours or days before Ham's body was found. Separating him from his comm link, or just turning it off, would have bought even more time for an escape."

"So, the murder wasn't a hit job?"

"Can't rule out murder for hire. Wouldn't be the first time a vet turned freelance killer. But this is a sloppy, first murder. No serious planning. No thought to a cover up. We keep some very nasty chemicals in that space. Some can burn off flesh and melt bones in seconds. A can of that stuff was perched on a shelf right above where Ham died. Pop it open and knock it over and Ham's gills are gone. No beating needed and all the clues we got from Ham's body would have been gone."

Farragut nodded. "You need to know who on the ship has seen combat or gotten the right training. I'll get you the files."

Johnny smiled slightly. "Thanks Skipper. I did that almost as soon as I learned I was coming aboard. Besides, you giving me access could blow my cover. Better I get it my way."

"Those records are encrypted," Farragut growled, anger surging at the security breach Johnny had just revealed.

Johnny nodded in agreement. "More fun that way." *And more expensive,* he added mentally. *I need to figure out an expense reimbursement plan for this investigation, but not one that Farragut sees. Better for me if he remains ignorant of the extent of my resources.*

Johnny heard Farragut literally growl. Clearly the information security leakage Andretti had just revealed was something he wanted to dig into. Then, his expression shifted, one corner of his mouth turned up in the faintest hint of a smile.

I bet I'm not going to like what's coming next, Johnny thought.

"Speaking of fun, finish your drink Andretti. I've got someone I want you to meet. I hear these guys are a barrel of laughs."

Whatever they were, Johnny knew, *they were about to become a new set of tools – or pipe bombs exploding his world.*

12. The Plumber's Apprentices

Johnny scowled suspiciously at the three Marines standing at parade rest in front of the Captain's desk as he and Farragut entered the Captain's Ready Room.

"Sir, Lieutenant Susan Dunning and Lance Corporals Henry Hess and Ibrahin Arnold. Reporting as ordered." The words shot out crisp and clear, like a rifle shot at dawn.

Dunning[9] looked like a recruiting poster. Her hair black, straight, and close cropped. Dark eyes with long lashes and arched brows, a button nose, full lips and a small, pointed chin. Clear complexion, fading hints of a suntan tinting her white skin. She was wearing a short-sleeved khaki shirt, blue trousers with a red stripe down the side, a single silver bar on each collar point. Above her left breast pocket jump wings, a dive helmet pin, expert rifle and pistol—plus a Purple Heart with three stars. She weighed maybe one-twenty-five tops.

Two enlisted men in urban camouflage utilities stood at attention nearby. All three were Caucasian, even Arnold, despite his first name.

---

[9] See Black Files: BF-U-008 Third Star Susan Dunning. Personnel file. Access Union

"At ease," Farragut shot back. All three resumed their position of parade rest. None of them looked 'at ease' to Johnny.

Hess might have been a redhead, far from the sun, his hair was light brown. Freckles played hide and seek on his broad, square face, sometimes they seemed right there, but when you looked at him in another angle, they were gone. His dark brown eyes looked out of place on the almost featureless square of his pale face. Even his eyebrows seemed to fade into transparency. He was broad shouldered for his height, only about five-eight, but he was fit, as were all the Marines.

Arnold might have been a brother to Dunning with his dark hair and clear skin. He was taller than the others, just over six feet, and slender in both body and face. His dark brows were flat above his eyes like the horizon of the sea at midday.

The two men were trying to keep their faces totally neutral, but Johnny caught the flicker of fear in their eyes. They could feel the executioner's axe in Farragut's voice. Junior enlisted men only ended up in front of Farragut for two reasons. They knew they weren't up for any awards. That only left judgment.

Johnny sauntered into the room and sat down, uninvited, in one of the two chairs in front of Farragut's desk.

"Mister Andretti, thanks for coming." Farragut sounded like he wasn't bothered in the least by Johnny's cavalier disregard for his rank. "I know this whole problem with Mister Hamilton being out of action is putting you in a bit of a bind, trying to cover both shifts, on call, and the special duties I've given you."

John's eyebrows went up. "Special duties?"

Farragut nodded. "Everyone knows you are working with the doctor to figure out what caused that weird intestinal problem that put Ham in quarantine. As the only guy who knows where all the water on this station goes to and comes from it's only natural I would have you help with that."

Johnny nodded, not saying a word. It was clear that Farragut was running with the cover story for what was happening.

"John Andretti, this is Lieutenant Susan Dunning and Lance Corporals Hess and Arnold." Johnny nodded at the three Marines. They stood as still as statues. "The Lieutenant tells me that Hess and Arnold have both volunteered to help you out with your plumbing work."

Johnny guffawed. "No offense Skipper, but if the Marines are helping me with the plumbing, I'm going to need a whole Company of them."

"Well, we can't spare you more than two, but why do you need more Mr. Andretti?"

"First off, these volunteers were likely volun-told. The most probable reason they got this duty is that they are a couple of shit-birds or goldbrickers who have been a beer cap in the Lieutenant's shorts. Now, Dunning can make her problems into my problems. On target so far?"

Johnny could see his answer in everyone's face. He went on.

"Their plumbing expertise is playing with each other's plumbing in the swamps of Parris Island. They will require my undivided attention to supervise, slash, train, slash, babysit, and they will likely make a cosmic-level C.F. of whatever I was stupid enough to ask, slash, tell them to do. Leading directly to my need for more help. The damage they do will likely require a whole Division of jarheads up here to unscrew things."

Deeper red coloration was beginning to creep up Dunning's neck from her collar toward her firmly clamped jaw. Johnny ignored it.

"Finally, if these two can manage to quickly learn to do the job with any degree of accuracy, I will need four of them to do what I am required to do in any given 24-hour day."

Farragut laughed aloud. "Mister Andretti, you're full of surprises. I hadn't imagined you knew enough Marine-speak to know the term C.F." Amusement twinkling his eyes, Farragut turned to Dunning with a mock look of reproof. "Lieutenant, are trying to foist off shit-birds onto Mr. Andretti?"

Dunning snapped to attention. The two Lance Corporals followed suit.

"No sir. Hess and Arnold volunteered because both have some hands-on experience with pipe fitting, sir." The red on her throat hadn't retreated a millimeter.

Andretti laughed aloud, confident that he was right.

"There you have it Mister Andretti. The Lieutenant says these men are qualified to help you. These two Marines are your new apprentice plumbers. If it turns out the Lieutenant has been blowing smoke, let me know. I'll have her and her two volunteers scraping off rust and painting every dusty, forgotten corner of the station, just the three of them."

Dunning shot Johnny a glance that let him know not only was he right, but she would happily shove him out an airlock, after breaking every bone in his body.

"Dismissed."

Johnny and the three Marines left Farragut's office. They marched, Johnny sauntered. They were waiting for him a short distance down the passageway.

Dunning looked ready to explode, the deeper red of her neck still flashing danger signals to the plumber. Johnny held up a hand, palm out to forestall her. "Truce?" He asked.

She swallowed whatever she had been about to say. Instead, she said, "What do you want?"

"I sincerely want someone to help with the plumbing work. Have you got anyone who actually might have fitted a pipe that wasn't a euphemism for having sex?"

"Ma'am," it was Hess, "if I may?"

Hess turned to Johnny. "You are right, and you are wrong about us."

"Go on."

"Arnold and I are," he paused for the right words, "not the best Marines in the platoon. Our boredom may have led us to some questionable activities." It seemed like the last was more of an apology aimed at Dunning.

"And," he continued when Dunning showed no acknowledgment of his apology, "I do know something about plumbing. I grew up on a farm and had to keep our irrigation systems up and running. Pulse scheduling, pressure loss over dirty runs. I can read flow like some folks read Psalms."

Johnny looked at the two men. He could see that they weren't happy with being pushed on him. He could see that Dunning felt she was now in a lose-lose situation.

"Lieutenant, let's make a deal."

"I'm listening," the red in her held steady.

"Barring something really screwed up, I will make sure that Farragut will hear only my praises for these two, and you. Any of their high jinks I can't handle will be your eyes only."

"So far, so good. What do you want in return?" the red in her neck retreated.

"Right now, I don't have much free time, but when I do, I would like to have access to some of your experienced Marines for some practice at hand-to-hand combat."

"Training?" The request clearly surprised her. "I suppose..."

"Not training. Practice."

That surprised her even more. She looked him over again, realizing for the first time that although he wasn't particularly tall, his coveralls pulled a bit tight across his shoulders and chest and there was no corresponding stress around the middle of his uniform. "Practice?"

"Assuming that part of your efforts to combat the boredom is to make your Marines train and practice until they are doing it in their sleep?"

"Of course." It was clear that was not exactly the case.

"Good. If you can send Hess and Arnold to me every day right after morning chow, I will fill their days until they can fix pipes in their sleep."

"Perfect."

"When can I have them?"

"Right now."

"Good. You two, with me." Johnny strolled off down the passageway. With a "By your leave, Sir," to Dunning, they fell in behind Johnny.

"You two know where the Plumbers Closet is?"

"Yes sir."

"Get into coveralls and wait for me there. I have something I need to do right now." *Now, I'm training people who are informing on me.*

"Andretti, be careful with my Marines. You break 'em, I break you," Dunning warned.

Training informants. Using Marines as snitches. Johnny knew he'd crossed more lines for less payoff.

This one, at least, might keep everyone breathing.

Act III Water, Guns, and Ghosts

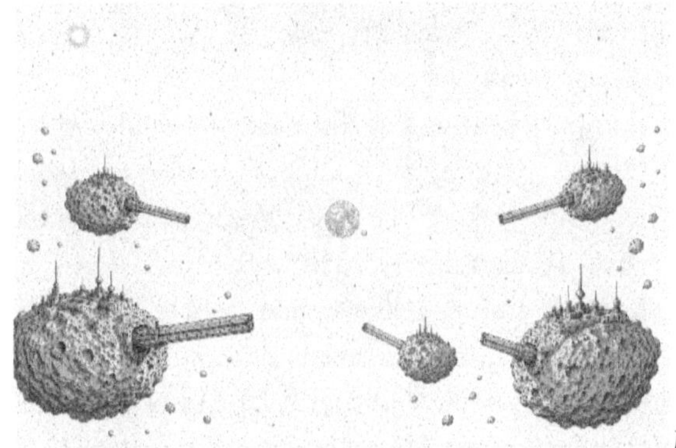

Figure 3

The Shooting Gallery

13. Not a Drop to Drink

Johnny dropped off the service ladder to Deck Sixteen with a wrench in his pocket and sweat cooling on his neck. Night-cycle dimmed the passage lights to a tired glow. Good for sleeping, bad for spotting trouble. He let his eyes blur and scanned edges and negative space. Twenty paces ahead a faint star field of beads dotted the overhead rib. Too uniform for a spill. Not a transient hiccup.

He set a breadcrumb on his wrist. *Frame 437.* Bulkhead watermark led him to a hatch with fresh yellow stencil: WATER STORAGE — SERVICE ONLY. New paint, old wheel. He spun it and cold air brushed his cheeks.

Potable ran warm of ambient on paper. This was an icebox. "Too cold," he murmured.

This little icebox was stealing from somewhere and leaking it into his hallway. *The colder the steel, the hotter the lie. Ships don't waste Joules.*

The compartment was coffin-narrow—standard vertical cylinder, access grating, two inspection ports at shoulder height, a control stack on the right. Foam insulation banded the tank like a baker had iced it with a bad wrist: seams gapped, a patch slumped like it had been slapped on and forgotten. A low-bidder had loved and left this one.

Johnny put his palm to the tank. The steel hummed with mass. Not empty, then. He tapped two knuckles. The note came back slow and deep.

"You're not the ten-thousand," he told it. "You're your big sister in a smaller dress."

He unclipped the infrared and blinked at the readout: 3.8°C on the shell, maybe a degree warmer up top. The pipe outfeed showed five warmer, but the infeed line frost-kissed its bracket. He swore under his breath. Frost on a drinking water loop. The Odyssey would have him whipped with a hose if she could talk.

He set down the bucket and drew a bead of spray foam across the worst seam. The foam hissed, swelled, and smoothed under the paddle like meringue. He moved along the banding, patching, smoothing, re-skinning the lazy work with clean layers. The hiss and tap-tap of the paddle filled the compartment, a white-noise steady enough to let the mind wander. It wandered straight to Ham's face, or what was left of it, and then to Bay Sixteen, three inches of bulkhead away and a mile out of reach.

When the last seam was sealed, the compartment air felt less like winter was coming and more like early spring. He checked the frame again—5.1°C. Better. He worked the infeed bracket loose, wrapped it, then refit the clamp with a strip of vapor barrier underneath to keep the steel from sweating. He took a step back and gave it the kind of look he used to give a dead man to make sure the job was done.

The control stack blinked at him, green and smug. A neat little digital here-and-now: TANK 16-0R-27 / STATUS: FULL / VOL: 10,000 L / TEMP: 5°C.

Johnny frowned. Ten-thousand liters at five degrees was a lot of cold water for a ship that ran warm loops and chased every wasted Joule like it owed rent. He pulled the tablet plate forward and dropped the service flap. The internals were standard: a local controller, a relay bus for the manifold, two redundant volumetrics, a stupid little b-flat buzz from the step-down transformer they taught kids to ignore.

He went into maintenance mode on his wrist and jacked the unit with a patch cable. The control stack tried to be coy and asked for a password. Johnny let the timer spin while he looked at the tank itself.

"Show me your body honey," he said, circling. The tank footprint ran longer than his memory of the spec sheet. The supports were doubled up. The inspection ports were taller by a hand. He stopped and measured off the radius with his shoulder and hand like an old carpenter—forearm to fingertip, elbow to wrist, two-and-a-quarter lengths for a standard ten thousand, call it a hair over a meter radius. What he had here was… "Three arms, easy," he said. "You're a fat girl in your skinny kid-sister's cut offs."

The controller chirped. Maintenance accepted. Johnny flicked through the menu tree, found CALIBRATION / VOLUME, and pulled up the curve. In the simple world, volume rose with height and the software did integrals a child could recite with their colors. In the real world, people lied to computers and computers lied for them.

The lookup table seemed ordinary enough—levels mapped to liters in a neat array. What wasn't neat was the display logic: whoever wrote this had simply clamped the report at the "full" default instead of letting it continue to count. Once the level hit 10,000 the routine stopped and substituted the default value for any higher reading—no incrementing, no summation, no alarm. Johnny scrolled down to the raw sensor feed and his eyebrows rose. The sensor itself read 39,402 L. The controller, obedient to its sloppy defaults, was cheerfully telling the ship it had ten thousand.

Johnny sat on the grating and laughed once, a hard bark that died in the cold air.

"Jurassic Park," he said. "Count the raptors to you expect, then stop and swear they're not breeding."

He tore off the cap, toggled the ALARM IF CAP EXCEEDS SPEC flag to IGNORE, and backed out to the display. The local screen hiccuped and then blossomed a number that didn't belong on any spec sheet: 39,401 L. The status still said FULL because someone had set full to >= CAP and never thought to make it pretty.

He took a still of the screen with his wrist and killed the local beeper before it could think to squeal to central. Then he went hunting.

Odyssey fed all her utility reporting through a mid-deck aggregator before sending it to the bridge. Johnny had grumbled his way into read-only for it on day two because he was lazy and he liked to see the world in one scroll. Now he forked a little scrivener script to scrape the potable subsystem—every tank, every manifold, every outflow, the tempering loops, the recycling return. The data arrived clean and stupid: a dozen tanks like his cheerfully reporting ten-thousand liters, never less, never more, always full like the Lord's cup on a good day.

He pushed the same trick to three more locals. All three coughed and then confessed: 41,227 L, 38,990 L, 42,105 L. The aggregator still sang ten-thousand hymns.

He opened the reporting routine. It wasn't sloppy; it was pretty. Someone had tested it, someone had commented it, someone had put in fail safes and then aimed them the wrong way. If a tank reported more than spec, the routine stopped counting at spec. If a sum exceeded design capacity, the routine substituted design capacity. If you asked why, the log would tell you it was a "valid range enforcement," a phrase that meant don't look here.

Johnny set a second script to mirror the raw values without touching the pretty reports and tucked it under a harmless maintenance header that would look like a leak-rate test to anyone not nosy. He let it run five minutes while he patched one more sloppy seam with foam and listened to the hiss.

Raw numbers stacked inside his wrist like coins. He had to resist the urge to whistle.

He pivoted to outflows. If the thieves he'd chased were tapping pressure and leaving volume alone, it meant the system masked the theft exactly the way he'd just watched it mask surplus. The outflow logs were messy by design; water went everywhere—galley, hydroponics, laundry, showers, scrubbers. He filtered for events labeled EJECTION because idiots label crimes as crimes and honest men label them as MAINTENANCE. The ejection log had four entries in the last ninety days, all tagged with the same location stamp: HANGAR SUB—B16. No volumes attached, just a checksum and a timing stub: hatch closed, vent opened, vent closed.

He looked at the bulkhead. It looked back.

"Bravo-One-Six," he said softly. On comms he would have given it the phonetics. Alone, he gave it his breath.

He cross-checked with exterior maintenance. The ship kept a registry of parked debris—broken panels, dead drones, storage pods. The registry had a tidy list of ICE HOLD—AFT with half a dozen entries in the last quarter. Each one had a mass noted and a tether ID. Each one built a picture: field ice harvested, tugged in, caged, left to wait.

He pulled the hydroponics logs. Temperatures had dipped twice in the last month with no schedule. Water quality had pinged at the margin for dissolved organics despite the scrubbers doing their job. A cold slug had passed the plants and asked them to like it. They didn't.

Johnny felt the grin before he realized it was on his face. He tamped it down. Smiles were tells. He learned that the same day he learned to sit with his back to a wall and a gun under the table.

He put the control stack back together and sealed the service flap. The compartment held its chill, but the condensation in the corridor would ease once the foam cured. He lingered a second, the way he always lingered at the edge of a job to see if he'd missed anything. Then he stepped out and spun the wheel shut, leaving the new stencil to lie for him if anyone asked. He harvested the condensation and moved on.

Back in the passage he leaned his shoulder to the bulkhead and scrolled the raw mirror. A one-hour window charted across his wrist in clean slope: total potable volume, by raw sensors, up three percent since he'd started breathing in this corner of the ship. If he layered the last week, the slope ran steady with dips where usage spiked and something else that wasn't usage at all—sharp notches where volumes vanished without moving through any registered outflow. The notches lined up within minutes of the EJECTION tags.

"Bread and circuses," he told the steel. "But mostly bread. And a tithe to the priest."

He didn't ping Farragut. The Captain's comms were hungry these days and Johnny had no taste for feeding a predator twice in one night. He rolled up the scripts, set them to keep mirroring raw to a file only he could see, and hid a second copy behind an innocuous temperature calibration header where only a plumber would ever look.

On his way back toward hydroponics he cut through a maintenance chase that ran behind the hangar sub-bays. The hum there was different—more muscle, less bone. Voices carried oddly where steel boxed them in: a laugh with no warmth, a woman's murmur, boots in a pair. He slowed and let his footfalls match the rhythm of the pump. At a branch he stopped, bent down, and fiddled with a valve that didn't need fiddling while his ears did their own work.

The voices went past. He caught the words "load" and "shift" and "window." He caught the soft click of a sidearm safety put off and on again, like someone reminding their finger it wasn't time to twitch.

Johnny waited until the hum swallowed them, then moved on. He forced his mind to the job in front of him: hydroponics had blown a gasket earlier and he had a replacement in his thigh pocket. He had real work to do or the cover he'd been given would peel at the edges like old tape.

Hydroponics smelled like salad and soil and the sour of men. The long troughs winked with dew; fans whispered like they were sharing a secret. The chief grower, a narrow-shouldered civilian who looked like he'd lost an argument with a lamp, nodded without looking up from his tablet. The Monsanto patch on his shoulder marked him as a civilian. One of thousands of big business employees cast off to the edges of space to squeeze money out of a government contract to create agribusiness in low-g.

"You're late."

"I'm on time. Your clock's wrong," Johnny said, and he meant it; he'd seen the man's clock drift two minutes a day. He popped the panel beneath a lettuce wall and swapped the blown gasket by feel. He bled off the air and let the loop fatten with flow.

"Hey," the grower said, eyes still on his screen, "we had two cold snaps this week. You people change something?"

Johnny kept his head down. "No. You get condensation?"

"In the returns. Leaves got mad. We lost a tray."

Johnny grunted. He looked up through the slats of green. A row of baby butterheads had gone yellow on the edge like Jack Frost had breathed on them. He made the appropriate noises and closed the panel.

On his wrist the raw tally ticked upward another hair, steady as a heartbeat. He watched it like a pit boss watches a back room and thought of a different room, a different table, a different game. Tommy the Greek used to say there were only three questions that mattered in any job: Who feeds? Who bleeds? Who counts?

The Odyssey had been feeding. Someone else had been bleeding. And the ship had not been counting; she'd been told not to. He'd just taught her to count again and the numbers said what his nose and knuckles already knew.

Space was not empty. It was wet.

He finished the hydroponics ticket and logged the job with the same surly shorthand he always used so the Chief Engineer wouldn't think he was trying to impress anyone. Then he turned down a maintenance spur and keyed open a tiny service hatch nobody used unless they were cleaning ducts. It dropped to a crawlspace that ran between the hangar's inner bulkhead and the main water trunks. It wasn't on the tourist map. It was on his.

Halfway down, he reached a port the size of a dinner plate set into the bulkhead. Somebody had brushed gray over its rim and face without looking. He thumbed the latch. It wouldn't open; someone had welded it shut along the inside seam. He smiled without humor and patted the steel like you pat a dog you don't trust.

He tapped the wrist to life one more time and pulled up a new page he'd coded while the foam cured: WATER—RAW / INVENTORY / EVENTS. The inventory read +18% OVER DESIGN. The events list scrolled; two ejections last month, two ice holdings parked aft, one short ejection three days ago timed just after the meteor drill. A neat little "coincidence."

He added a line: NOTE: 16-0R STORAGE ADJ B16—TANKS OVERSPEC / REPORT CAPS HARD-CODED / MIRROR ONGOING.

He closed the hatch and slid out of the crawlspace. As he straightened, he saw his reflection in a stainless panel: tired eyes, unremarkable face, coveralls with a new smear of foam on the thigh. Forgettable. He'd built his life on that. It worked just as well in space.

On the way to the ladder he passed a porthole the size of his hand. Most crew ignored them—they were like peepholes into the same dark night, the same fixed stars—but Johnny looked because looking was the difference between walking out and being carried. Far aft and low, where the Odyssey's shadow cut a wedge in the dust-light, something glinted—a pale, lumpy sphere riding a tether like a dog on a leash. Beyond that, farther still, a cluster of smaller shapes drifted at the edge of the floodlights, patient as stones.

Gift-wrapped, he thought. The good stuff always leaves wrapped.

He climbed the ladder, the raw tally ticking up on his wrist with each rung, and let the ship hum to him like a distant bar with a door half-open, music you only hear if you listen. He would tell Farragut—later, in the right room, with the right door shut. First, he'd finish the plumbing. It was the cover and the work, and tonight, they were the same thing.

Thinking about the sudden reality of the abundance of water, he laughed to himself. "Water, water everywhere, and not a drop to drink." Coleridge had nailed it more than two centuries too early. The irony was brutal. The tanks were bursting, a string of frozen spheres tethered outside, and the ship still rationed showers and banned ice cubes.

Johnny smiled to himself. This racket was about to get really fun, and lucrative. *My expense account on this investigation just found the right bank account.* As soon as he found Ham's killer and connection, he was going to start scaling this operation. He hoped the killer wasn't his connection. That would complicate things.

Hess and Arnold were waiting for him outside the door of the Plumber's Closet. Lafferty's security feed had notified him of their arrival nearly an hour earlier.

"Finally. We've been waiting here for nearly two hours." Hess whined. Clearly, they had wasted an hour somewhere between getting his orders and showing up for duty.

"Instead of swapping uniforms and beating feet here, you two dicked-off somewhere for most of an hour. Thought you'd keep me waiting on you? Not a good start boys."

They said nothing.

"On your own time, I don't care, but you two shit-birds can forget your fun and games while you're on my dime."

Hess opened his mouth, Arnold elbowed him in the ribs. "Mr. Andretti, we appreciate this opportunity. Thank you. We're eager to get started."

"Call me John. If we become friends, you can call me Johnny. Until then, John or Andretti will do." Johnny touched his wrist unit and those of Hess and Arnold both chimed. They looked automatically.

"Condensation?" Hess queried. "You want us to look for little drops of liquid?"

"Search every inch of this ship and note every place you see so much as a molecule of liquid that isn't in a containment tank. That includes all the common heads and the personal quarters of every crew member from the Skipper down to the lowest galley hand."

"The Skipper's quarters, that's a joke, right?" Arnold.

Johnny smiled. "Start there. Stick together. Be thorough. Every square inch. Work it like a white-glove inspection. And give the Skipper my regards."

Every square inch. White-glove it. Because whatever they missed now, they'd end up choking on later.

14. The Investigation Expands

Toolkit in hand, Johnny was crossing the hangar deck when the "incoming ship" klaxon sounded. He paused to watch. Surreptitiously, he tapped his modified wrist unit and began recording.

The interior side of the heavy hangar doors were rigged with thin screens which showed the view into the landing dock and the space beyond. A mid-size freighter, fully illuminated for landing was approaching the landing dock. In the distance, Johnny could see a cluster of cargo containers, parked to one side of the docking lane. Patiently waiting for the next stage of their journey.

At first, the freighter seemed to be spinning slightly, then it stabilized and aligned. The reality, Johnny knew, was that it was the station that was whirling and the incoming ship had to adjust to match. Even without the ocean beneath her keel, Odyssey had her own yaw, pitch, and roll that incoming craft had to match to land safely.

The freighter aligned and fired reverse thrusters as it slunk into the landing dock. One final blast of attitude thrusters pushed it to settle on the deck where guided tow cables shot out and grasped the sides of the freighter hull, securing it to the landing pad. The outer bay doors closed behind the freighter. The atmosphere cyclers pumped air into the dock, and then the inner bay doors opened, replacing the thin-screen view with the less dramatic, unmagnified appearance of the freighter. A mule, a small but powerful tractor, forced the freighter pads onto grav-lift platforms and began to drag the freighter deeper into the hangar.

Traffic control parked the freighter not far from where Johnny stood watching the show. He waited to see the next act.

The freighter's crew hatch opened along with the doors to the hold. Neatly dressed civilian passengers exited the crew hatch; the suits in charge. Through the now open hold marched a double column of dirty and bedraggled civilian miners. Johnny estimated around 300 men and women, all dressed in dirty work uniforms of the mining company concession they worked for.

Johnny tasted burnt rock in the air. It set his teeth a little on edge and jangled his nerves. It called out like the welcoming fires of Hell Father Mark's sermons promised were the reward for bad little girls and boys. He looked closely at the miners. This didn't look at all like a modern version of the rough-and-tumble wild bunch miners from the gold rush days of the old West. The double column of civilians didn't exactly march in time, but they didn't straggle like a mob of civilians either. They were orderly. Too orderly. And uniform.

No exotic hairstyles or colorful gear. All seemed to be outfitted with the same large duffel bag and pack, slung onto their shoulders the packs bulged in all the same places. Hanging from their hands, the duffels were almost all of the same size. The grime on some seemed to settle on the stenciled names of the owners and also on phantom words and symbols beneath and around the company logos stenciled there, like dust on paper where something has been erased.

The miners and hangar crew didn't interact much. A few greetings, nods of acknowledgement, or waves. In front of Bay 16, the Marines working there met their gazes and nodded at one another or waved with much more frequency than came from the Space Force personnel. That was when Johnny noticed that many of the miners sported overgrown versions of the same high-and-tight Marine haircut.

Johnny made a mental note for later entry in his private log: *Marines and mining engineers equals fortified combat posts.*

After the last of the miners exited the freighter a maintenance crew quickly moved in. No undue haste, just the speed and precision of a NASCAR pit crew, of forty people. They briskly cleaned and inspected the freighter, jotting their actions and results on checklists projected on-demand from their wrist units. Assuming the show was over, Johnny picked up his bag again when a new sound greeted him.

It felt a bit like watching a movie playing in reverse as a fresh group of about 300 miners tramped into the hangar deck in a double column, uniformly lumpy packs on their back and duffels hanging from their hands and into the freighter; contingent of 'suits' off to one side.

The suits from the dirty miners faced off with the suits from the fresh crew. They exchanged data from their wrist units, chatting amiably remaining space in the hold was filled with pallets of crates; shrink wrapped to prevent shifting. Labels indicating everything from food rations and entertainment vids, to specialized mining equipment and spare parts.

When the freighter's cargo doors clanged shut the set of suits split in two; one group following the same path the dirty miners had taken before them. The other group fell into a double column until they reached the passenger hatch of the freighter. The suit-in-charge suit stepped through first and first one column, then the other group of suits followed through the hatch.

Moments later, the 'outgoing craft' klaxon sounded. The mules dragged the freighter back to the loading dock. The inner doors shut, with the thin screens again showing the action as air was pumped out of the landing dock and the outer doors opened to space. Of those in the hangar, Johnny was one of the few watching the departure of the freighter.

The batch of containers the freighter had parked outside the station appeared to be still there. Inexplicably, the freighter reconnected the container sled and then began moving away.

Two Marines in grease-stained coveralls stepped close behind Johnny. "Show's over plumber. Time to move on."

Johnny turned to face them, sizing them up and then reading their name tags and rank insignia carefully. "Gunnery Sergeant Zheng and," he turned to the second Marine, "Sergeant Beaumont, thank you both for showing up to assist me." Johnny tapped his wrist unit and a work order sprang into view into the space between the three men. "Let's go have a look at that balky toilet in the Bay Sixteen head. Shall we?" He smiled disarmingly while they examined his work order.

"Hess or Arnold can take care of that. Aren't they assigned to you?"

Johnny nodded amiably. "Yes, both those Marines are probably able to get that toilet working properly. However, as you mentioned, they are assigned to me and currently, they are carrying out my orders far from this part of Odyssey. So, we can go now and fix this. Or," Johnny shrugged, "if the toilet backs up all over the head, I will be sure to mention you both by name when I file my report to Captain Farragut. I will request you both personally as the two-man work detail that will spend four hours sucking up overflow into containment bags." Johnny shrugged. "Your call."

At that moment Chief of the Deck Marissa Lowman, and Lieutenant Dunning[10] appeared. Both women carried the air of command comfortably.

"You three," Chief Lowman growled. "Get your asses elsewhere, or get to work. No spectators on my hangar deck."

---

[10] See Black Files: BF-U-009 The Lieutenant in Bay Sixteen. Access: Union

"Chief. Lieutenant." Beaumont acknowledged. "We were just now redirecting this civilian."

Johnny pointed to the work order, still visible. Both Dunning and the Chief examined it quickly.

"Gunny Zheng," Dunning snapped. "Is there some reason you aren't escorting the plumber to his work?"

Zheng shot Dunning a questioning look. "Sir, we thought Arnold or Hess would be handling a routine matter like this," he paused a micro-beat, "in Bay Sixteen."

"Andretti, why aren't they handling this?" Dunning fired at Johnny.

"They're where I told them to be, doing what I told them to do." Johnny's tone was a flat iron bar across the conversation. No bend. No flex. No further explanation offered.

Sergeant Beaumont's hand shot out, grabbing Johnny by the front of his shirt, jerking the plumber around to face him. "Listen you scum sucking sewer rat. You'll speak respectfully to the Lieutenant and the Chief, or you'll be gumming your next meal."

"Sergeant." Dunning and Lowman both spoke together. A cannon shot, two guns of the same caliber snapping a verbal bullet into the head of Sergeant Beaumont, formerly of the French Foreign Legion. Instantly he released Johnny and snapped to attention.

Dunning shoved herself roughly between Johnny and the Sergeant. Johnny swore standing next to her felt like standing beside a glacier in summer. The cold burned. Her eyes were narrowed, gunsights locked on target, finger on the trigger, firing point blank. Taller than her, the Sergeant stared straight ahead, about six inches above Dunning's head.

"Look. At. Me. Sergeant." Her voice a whisper, the warning hiss of a snake before striking. Beaumont's head tilted down with the crisp precision of a swivel. "You see these?" she pointed to the dive helmet and jump wings on her chest.

"Yes sir."

"It's been a minute since the Legion was absorbed into the Corps. Do I need to explain what they mean?"

"No sir."

Her head shifted forward by a millimeter. The inbound round was about to impact. The suppressed fury in her voice was evident. "Is there anything about those badges that suggests I needed your rescue? Do you think I pop a MAYDAY or PAN-PAN in the face of a mouthy civilian?"

"No sir."

"I know how, and when, to request reinforcement or bombardment. I'll excuse your behavior this one time because your Legionnaire training might have kicked in before you had a chance to think this through." Her head slid back a millimeter. Kill strike averted. "However, I don't know if the only working civilian Master Plumber we have on board is as forgiving as I. He might want to press charges. Mister Andretti?" The last was fired at the plumber without looking his direction.

"Lieutenant," he replied quietly, "is there something about my uniform that suggests I needed *your* rescue?"

Dunning turned around, facing Johnny. Her expression was a mixture of fury and disbelief. Before she could give voice to her thoughts, Chief Lowman stepped forward offering her hand to Johnny.

"Mister Andretti. I don't believe we've been introduced. I'm Senior Master Chief Marissa Lowman, Chief of the Deck." Although the title of Chief was a military designation, Lowman wore it like she was born to the title. She was a chief, regardless of rank. South African Zulu by ancestry, her bearing telegraphed a clear message – warrior, leader, lion.

Johnny returned the handshake. She gripped his hand firmly, fiercely, respectfully. "It's a pleasure to meet you Chief."

"If I read Captain Farragut's memo correctly, you are serving as Chief Fluids Engineer for Odyssey?"

"Yes ma'am."

Lowman smiled, a dazzling white flash of teeth, dimples in her cheeks and a spark in her liquid brown eyes that took Johnny's breath away for a moment. "I work for a living Mister Andretti. The UER dropped the ma'am, and you should never say sir when talking to an enlisted," she quietly corrected his error. "Just call me Chief."

"Chief," he agreed with a small nod.

Lowman nodded. "Good. Now, I hope you can clarify something for me."

"Happy to try."

"As the Chief of Fluid Engineering on the Odyssey, doesn't that put you on an even organizational footing with a senior enlisted, or an officer?"

"I hadn't considered that Chief. Does it?"

"According to the T-O, you are filling the billet of a Lieutenant Commander, an O4. Essentially a number two spot in Engineering." Lowman smiled again. "My apologies. Civilians on a military command always confuse me. I looked it up when the memo came across my desk."

Lowman glanced at Zheng and Beaumont. "Civilians can be dangerous when it comes to rank. With us," she waved a hand at the people around Johnny, "we see rank on collar points, sleeves, or plackets. With civilians, rank is hidden behind a stack of papers."

"I guess that could be a sort of minefield, couldn't it?" Johnny agreed.

Lowman nodded in agreement, "a minefield is an excellent analogy. Or, firing from concealment, sir."

Johnny unleashed his most dazzling smile, something he seldom did. "Chief, regardless of the Table of Organization, I work for a living too. Please, don't 'sir' me. Andretti is fine, or I would take it as a personal favor if you called me Johnny."

"Johnny sounds nice," she agreed. "However, I'll keep it to Mister Andretti, if you don't mind. I don't want any lax discipline on my deck. Don't you agree?"

Johnny's eyes twinkled back at Lowman. "I understand that discipline is important aboard ship."

"And a brawl in my hangar would be the antithesis of discipline. Don't you agree?" Lowman patted Johnny on the arm. "Mister Andretti, please, be a dear and let these Marines keep you safe while you," she glanced back at the work order, still projected from Johnny's wrist unit, "do battle with the misbehaving toilet in Bay Sixteen."

"My pleasure Chief." Tossing another smile at Lowman, Johnny turned and started for the opening to Bay 16.

"What are you two waiting for?" Dunning snapped at Zheng and Beaumont. "Carry on."

The slow toilet required no more than the proper use of a plunger. No smelly cleanup and no drama. Zheng and Beaumont glared at Johnny the whole time. When Johnny was done, he turned to them.

"Sorry about all that on the hangar deck, gents. Spending my days up to my elbows in this crap," he pointed meaningfully toward the toilet, "sometimes makes me a bit testy. I know you're just doing your jobs. We good Gunny?" Johnny offered his hand toward Zheng.

Zheng took the offered hand. "We might have come on a little too strong. Orders are to keep folks away … um away from anywhere they shouldn't be or where they might get hurt. Sorry." Johnny took note of his reference to orders to keep folks away, probably away from Bay 16.

Johnny extended his hand to Beaumont. "We good Sergeant?"

Beaumont nodded and shook his hand.

"Truth? I had no idea about all that Table of Organization stuff Chief Lowman mentioned."

"So, you were just dissing the LT because you could?" Beaumont stiffened.

Johnny's head bobbed to the side slightly, a sort of shrug. "No disrespect. Just a command issue. She pawned those two goldbrickers, Hess and Arnold, off on me. Reads like a transfer to me. Now, she questions what I'm doing with them?" He shook his head. "Not her call anymore. That didn't sit well with me."

Beaumont thought about it a moment, then nodded.

"You boys drink any of that bug-juice the Cook's helper is brewing?" He knew they did.

Both Marines stiffened a bit at what could have been an admission of breaking regulations.

Johnny, wiped the words out of the air with a wave of his hand. "Forget I asked." He punched a couple of buttons on his wrist unit and a small chip popped out. Universal, untraceable cash on the Odyssey. He pulled it out and offered it to Beaumont. "Peace offering? Slip this to the Kitchen Weasel and get your next round on me." Untraceable was a bedtime story. But it helped men sleep.

"Kitchen Weasel," Zheng smiled. "The name suits him."

Beaumont smiled and took the chip. "He's KW in my book from now on."

Back in his 'lair,' Johnny studied the recording he had made of the events in the hangar. With a little work, he enhanced the 'erased' images on the miners' duffels. At first, he thought it was a capital 'E'. Then, it dawned on him that being, creatures of habit, the replacement stenciling wouldn't likely run at right angles to the old stencil. That was when he saw that it looked like a castle. Two crenelated towers with a third, shorter one in the middle, over top a gate. Within seconds, the computer told him that it was the emblem of the Army Corps of Engineers.

The Army's working the Belt? Johnny asked the air. According to all the public records, mining rights for the asteroid belt had been auctioned. Mining companies from all over the world won claims. Each laid claim to a sector of the Belt and began working their claims. Unlike historical gold rushes, this was no wild west. The UER was firmly controlling this frontier.

Odyssey was the jumping off point for all miners, regardless of their sector. The media continued to spin stories of thousands of civilian miners jubilantly and tirelessly working to bring the wealth of the Belt to benefit the people of Earth. Meanwhile, the reality was the Army Corps of Engineers was working the Belt under cover of being mining company employees. *Is there a payroll scam in there? Or do the 'miners' get one check from the* UER *and another from the mining company?* Johnny smirked. *Odds are there's skimming in a double-pay play. Just like many union jobs back home.*

He pinned that to his mental board and moved on to the container sled mystery.

Studying close-ups as well as pics from before and after he quickly realized the container sleds were swapped while the freighter was parked in the hangar. Answering one question led to another. What was in the containers.

The story told by the official records was predictably boring. Mining companies chartered a fleet of freighters like the Sally Ann to drag empty containers, and some supply containers, along with fresh miners out to the Belt and bring back tired miners and containers full of ore. The Moon was the industrial hub for most of the ore processing. That meant there was one chain between Earth and Luna, another from Luna to Odyssey, and a third from Odyssey to the Belt.

Johnny knew that container shipping and dock workers were like magnets for organized crime for smuggling, theft, and fraud. *No reason for the rules to change in space,* he reasoned.

And those logistical chains, Johnny smirked, That's plenty of highway for things to 'fall off the truck.' Or, he realized, for off-book cargo to slip onto a sled.

In addition to crossing checking official manifests, he slid past the Skipper's communications block, dropping a quiet line, along with the requisite payments, to his network back on Earth.

Greasing the wheels of the information highway was often expensive, especially when it crossed from SIGINT to HUMINT. Hacking signals could be expensive, but it was usually much cheaper than turning people into information conduits. Seeing his accounts drop, he thought, *If this investigation doesn't flip into real profit, my retirement fund is going to be wiped out.*

When the facts and hints rolled back in Johnny assembled the big picture. He was gobsmacked. He dropped a simple entry into his encrypted log: *This racket is industrial scale. Strike that. Governmental scale.*

Johnny didn't sleep. He watched the ship roll from night-cycle to day and decided he'd had enough of numbers. Pipes lied quiet. People leaked.

Hess and Arnold caught up to him in the passage outside Stores with the eager faces of men who think they've done something heroic.

"Moisture inspection completed, sir," Arnold reported. "Including the Captain's quarters."

"How'd that go?" Johnny asked, deadpan.

Hess rubbed the back of his neck, grinning slightly. "The Skipper didn't flinch. He nodded and headed for the Bridge. The XO looked like he'd swallowed a wrench when we showed him our orders. We told him you wanted a white-glove check for condensate. He said, 'In my cabin?' We said, 'Yes, sir.' He watched us while we inspected the shower, the vents, and the underside of his teacups."

"Find anything?"

"Not even a teardrop," Arnold said. "But the XO sweats when he's angry."

"Good," Johnny said. He looked over the rest of their results highlighting a couple of specific areas. "Dig deeper in these areas. See if you can find evidence of persistent condensation or leaks. One more thing," He added. Then, he sent them off with a fresh tasking—map where the crew actually lived when they weren't on the clock—and swung down to the mess with his toolbox, the universal passport of a man nobody wanted to stop.

"Now let's look for the kind of leaks that wear boots."

The galley sprayer stuck on the third squeeze, same as yesterday. The galley hand glared at it like it had insulted his mother.

Johnny twisted the nozzle free, dug out a crescent of grit with his pick, and let the spray run clean. He didn't hand it back. Just let the water hiss, steady and wasteful, the kind of thing that would get a galley hand written up and slapped with an NJP – the non-judicial punishment that his commanding officer could hand out.

"Sprayers jam when they get grit," Johnny said conversationally. He clicked the head twice, sharp splats on the steel. "People jam when they owe. Ham ever run you a tab before now?"

The kid froze. Too long. His eyes moved back and forth and he squirmed slightly, like a weasel ready to bolt. Johnny could smell the answer before the boy's lips moved.

"Just ice," the kid muttered. "Couple cubes, now and then. For my girl. You know how it is."

Johnny's eyes didn't move off him. The hiss of water filled the silence.

Kitchen Weasel shifted on his feet, eyes darting for somewhere else to land. Johnny let the silence stretch, the spray still hissing between them.

Finally, the kid cleared his throat. "I'm not scared." It came out too quick. He looked down, then back up.

The kid's eyes skittered and he swallowed once, twice, a third time. "Ham… he was always swapping shifts. Nights, mostly. Said he liked the quiet. Took walks down by the hangar after mess. That's where I'd catch him—slip him the chits, he'd slip me the cubes." He shifted his weight. "Last week he said he was close to a transfer. Needed to close me out. Told me he would start flipping business to Rao. But he never looked like a man getting out."

Johnny shut the sprayer off, dropped it back in its bracket, and finally let the kid breathe. "Funny thing about tabs," he said, wiping his hands on a rag. "They never really close. Somebody always picks them up. You let me know the next time you need some ice to cool your ardor. But, be careful who you tell. If I get jammed up for this, you're going to experience some real pain. You feel me?"

Johnny turned to go, and then, making it look like an afterthought, he paused and half turned back to his Kitchen Weasel just as the boy was starting to relax. "Oh, by the way. If a couple of Marines show up here with a chit from me, looking for that rot-gut you're brewing in the back closet, treat them right. Ice and clean water too. Whatever they want. I'll take it off your tab. Understood?" Johnny didn't wait for Kitchen Weasel to reply. He left the galley hand staring at the sink, water still dripping like a clock counting down.

He cut through a service ladderwell and into a narrower artery of the ship where the paint never got freshened and conversation traveled better. He let the floor carry him. You didn't hunt panic; you set your hook and drifted until something hungry bit.

By midday-cycle, his wrist pinged—Hess. The Marines had made themselves useful, plotting smoke breaks like they were convoy routes. Clusters by the aft recycler. A quiet alcove near Hydro where three engineers rotated a deck of cards no one was supposed to have. And a corner on the hangar mezz where people who didn't like to be seen liked to stand.

Johnny made his rounds of the hot spots. Lafferty's rumor about investigating the plumbers for water theft had paved his way, and made folks more paranoid than usual. In his notebook, Ham had code named each gathering spot. Thanks to the information from his assistants, Johnny now had names, dates, and places to fill out his picture of Ham's business. He made it all his own. He and Ham were working together now. Nobody knew the Journeyman was dead. Everyone had heard he was sick.

Johnny's story was simple and natural. Like all good lies, it had grains of truth embedded.

"It happens," Johnny reassured them. "Messing with white-pipe sludge, it's almost inevitable to get the trots once in a while. Occupational hazard. This one's a bit harsh and not something Ham wanted to share. He's thoughtful that way. Feeling sick?" He paused, studying their faces, noting their names in his head. "Well, if you do, I'm sure it's nothing a nice shot of ice water wouldn't cure. Right?" He winked and started to walk away. Then he paused and turned back. "Oh, and while Ham is down, I'm delivering and collecting.

Don't be late or Lafferty might stumble onto your stash and make you stand tall in front of Farragut."

Johnny could almost hear the pressure ratchet up as he sauntered away.

Arnold came in on top of Hess' info with something better: a list from lost-and-found compiled by a bored ship's admin who posted orphaned badges in a tidy inventory. One badge kept disappearing and reappearing like a coin in a cheap trick.

Johnny shoved the report at the two Marines when Johnny met them in a junction nobody had reason to love. "You see anything odd here?"

Arnold studied the report. Confused at first that it wasn't about plumbing. Then, without questioning why he looked for anomalies.

"Rao's keycard almost never goes near B-Sixteen," Arnold said He held report pad like a catechism. He tapped the screen, bringing up some images. "But this orphan badge does—with Rao two paces behind it."

"Two paces?" Johnny asked.

Arnold nodded. "Different boots show up on camera, but he's always in frame." He tapped a still. "Same gait. Same shoulder hitch."

Hess snorted. "He thinks it's clever."

"It is clever," Johnny said. "Clever gets you ten minutes. Careless gets you dead."

They split again—Hess to keep tracing the ship's unofficial footpaths, Arnold to keep watching the badge churn. Johnny took a utility trunk toward Engineering to fix a "pressure chatter" that didn't exist and stopped halfway when something scratched into the paint caught his eye: a wave cresting over a broken link. Not neat. Not professional. Cut by a pocket tool, quick and dirty.

Hess arrived behind him, sweat-dark at the collar. "AguaLibre," he said. "That's their tag."

"You believe in bedtime stories?" Johnny asked. "This is about as far as you can get from an underwater dome in the Pacific Ocean. That's where all the stories say those gill-heads hide out."

Hess shrugged. "I believe in bored Marines and shaky civvies who like to tell them. 'Drowners in the drains,' they say—rebels who ran underwater after the unification. Figures they'd like a water line. Everyone likes cover."

Johnny brushed dust from the carving with the back of his glove. "Cover's only good if you don't carve your name in it," he said, but he took a still anyway and tucked the image into his private log. Propaganda traveled because someone wanted it to.

He set a "scheduled maintenance" that afternoon on a potable loop adjacent to the hangar sub-bays. The kind of test no one questioned: pressure verification, minor bleed, sign the form. It pulled exactly who he needed into a throat of corridor no wider than a coffin—Rao from Engineering, a hangar rigger with hands like mallets, and a thin hydro tech with eyes that flinched at fluorescent lights.

Johnny spun the valve a quarter-turn and let the gauge climb just enough to make the pipe sing.

"The trick with pressure," he said conversationally, "is you turn the dial until something talks. Ham taught me that."

Rao looked everywhere but at Johnny when he said Ham's name. The rigger kept lifting his chin to the corridor camera like it owed him approval. The hydro tech kept licking his lips and darting his eyes toward Bay 16 every time Johnny said "hangar." Johnny didn't need a notepad; he wrote with muscle memory. He bled the line back to spec and signed off the form, all neat and boring.

He walked the long way back to Hydro. On the way he ducked into a gray-water manifold closet to check on a rattle that didn't exist either and found a crate shoved behind a valve chest. Stencil said *Filters*. The weight said otherwise. He popped the lid and smiled without humor. No filters. Just rolls of insulation foam and a bale of welding curtains—the kind you used when you wanted to make a small room colder than it had any right to be, and you wanted to do it fast.

He checked the routing code. It terminated at 16-0R's access run. Adjoining Bay 16, like a polite knock on the devil's door.

Johnny shut the lid and thought about how men hid things. Not just bodies and money—heat. Cold was only heat turned around, and crooks hid heat every day. He slapped a bland maintenance tag on the crate and rerouted it to EVIDENCE—PERSONAL under a line item called

Inventory Normalization. The software yawned and moved the box on his say-so.

Outside, he ran into a wall in the shape of Commander Grigson.

"Maintenance," Johnny said, tipping his chin toward the corridor behind him.

"Your maintenance seems to cluster near the hangar," His voice had that slow, careful tone men used when they were balancing a glass on the sharpened edge of a knife.

"Maintenance clusters around leaks," Johnny tried to sound reasonable. "If you'd like them to cluster somewhere else, I'll have the ship moved."

Grigson's mouth twitched. "Captain Farragut would like you to report progress through proper channels."

"Farragut has my channels," Johnny said. "He also has my respect. Proper's extra."

They stared at each other for a second. Grigson broke first—not by looking away, but by looking through him, like a man who sees a cliff in fog and decides not to take the step today. He moved on.

Johnny waited until the echo of the XO's boots was gone and then kept going, slow and unimportant, a man with a wrench and a full day's work.

By the time night-cycle rolled around again, Hess had a map fit for a small war: smoke spots, card games, couples who thought the ship didn't see them. Arnold had fully mapped Rao and his orphan badge's movements. Three patterns appeared. One matched Rao's official duties and personal routines, along with his official badge. A second, an orphan shadowed part of Ham's 'business.' Another orphan they tied to Rao slithered in and around Bay 16—never at the same time every day, never on the same shift, but always within ten minutes of an "ejection window" logged in a system no one admitted existed.

"Rao seems to go where he pleases with his orphans," Arnold smirked.

"People will follow anything if you move it like you own it," Johnny said. "Even a ghost."

He dismissed them with a nod that said he wasn't unhappy, which was as close to "good work" as they were going to get. Then he found a piece of bulkhead that hummed at a frequency his bones liked and leaned against it while he scrolled what the day had given him.

Ham took "walks" by the hangar with not-Rao as a shadow. Rao walked behind a borrowed identity through Bay 16. Someone scratched a rebel mark into a Navy ship's skin. A crate of cold-making gear tried to sneak itself to 16-0R. And the human tells in a narrow corridor sang three different harmonies to the same melody: Bay 16.

The ship had stopped counting on purpose. Johnny had started counting again. Now the mouths were doing their part.

He closed his eyes long enough to taste metal and recycled mint on his tongue. The hum of the Odyssey ran through the panel and into his shoulder like a cat deciding whether to purr. Secrets stacked up on the far side of a bulkhead, patient as stored ice.

He pushed off the wall.

"If they want their curtains back," he told the air, "they'll come find me."

And because good hunters didn't wait in the same blind two nights in a row, he headed for a different corridor, a different job he didn't need to do, and a new angle on the door the whole ship pretended wasn't there.

He turned the corner and found Dunning waiting to ambush him. "Andretti, seems like you redirected a crate of filters inventoried for Bay Sixteen. I want 'em back. Right. Now."

"Sorry about little SNAFU. Give me the destination and I'll send it along," Johnny feigned chagrin. Dunning had come looking for the mis-labeled cold-making gear. In his mind Johnny immediately labeled her, The Ice Queen. *Has the water warped the Ice Queen into a Pirate Queen?*

"SNAFU or not. Don't touch Bay Sixteen gear. Ever," Dunning hissed.

15. Gun Running

Words matter, Johnny thought as he skimmed the "whispers" report his ghost sensors fed him. He had seeded pin mics in ventilation junctions, choke points in the corridors, and narrow pockets between bulkheads where ship noise braided together and carried voices like a wire. The feed rode through Odyssey's computers disguised as a sewage meter routine. To Engineering it looked like foam coefficients and flow curves. To Johnny it was a river of talk where he cast hooks, lines, and nets to catch the predators that lurked in the shadows of the stream.

His private AI did the first pass. Stripping out galley gossip and card-table lies, then floated the words that fit his hooks. He let the transcripts scroll while waveform ribbons pulsed beneath them.

The same family of words lit up again and again: range, tower, arc, node, emplacement, calibrate. "Tower Two hot," a whisper under fan noise. "Range markers to one-eighty-seven, confirm." "Power nodes arrive with the next load. Corps spec only." Corps. The castle kept surfacing in jokes and orders, that clipped respect men saved for engineers who built battlefields. Crate chatter shifted from drill heads to rail packages and capacitors. A loader hissed, "No one says howitzer on deck comms. Say rail." Another voice: "Stop calling them homesteads. They're emplacements until the towers stand." The AI overlaid tug telemetry on top of it all and sketched neat arcs across the Belt. Arc 3. Arc 7. Arc 12. A foreman snapped, "No civilians near calibration. If the Consuls want a demo, they'll get one on schedule." Demo for politicians. Guns dressed as logistics. Johnny felt the confirmation slide home like a well-oiled bolt. This was not mining. It was a ring of artillery built off the books.

Bay 16 did not fit as cleanly. It was a ripple from a pebble hitting the edge of the pond. His mics pulled phrases that tasted wrong in a gun plan: "sample integrity," "organics threshold," "no chemical contamination," "consignment complete." The gray lines hummed while a cold sphere sweated on the deck. Not a weapon, not a tower. A trade. He penciled it in as smuggler finance or heat cover for the gun drops. Crooks hid heat. Bureaucrats hid budgets. Either would explain a water shuffle during an ejection window.

Still, the pattern around the Belt was gospel to him now. Troop haircuts on "miners." Engineering Corps jargon on cargo lanes. Rail packages, power nodes, range markers marching in tidy arcs. The castle had its fingerprints everywhere except on the water scheme, which continued to throw little pebbles at the edge of his pond. He logged Bay 16 under Secondary Anomalies and moved the fortified ring to the center of the board. The coup picture sharpened. The water picture nagged. He told himself both could be true, but only one could topple a government. The guns came first. The drip could wait.

Seeing is believing, Johnny thought. The observation blister hid behind a maze of maintenance tunnels and a vacuum hatch no one remembered. Johnny loved it. The top of the blister was filled with devices feeding external observations to Odyssey's command center. Johnny rigged a row of thin-screen displays and a processor tapping the feeds. Adding a chair, he had as good a view of outside the ship as anyone on the Bridge. He could smoke without trouble, think without footsteps, and see the dark do business.

Two freighters approached on the same cycle. The laggard stood off the lock. While everyone's eyes were on the docking ballet, its bay doors cracked and several large containers slid into space and latched onto a waiting tether ring. Doors shut. The freighter fell back into queue.

A small tug, lights off, slid out of the dark, snagged the containers, cut the tether, and ghosted toward the Belt.

Johnny zoomed until letters resolved. Rail guns. Energy plants. Environmental conditioners. Add food and panel kits and you had an outpost in a box. Johnny captured the entire event, replaying it repeatedly. He opened his personal log and noted: *More than mining in the Belt. Building forts.*

Cybersecurity on Odyssey was built like a watertight bulkhead. Distance from Earth made people sloppy, not the system. Johnny leaned on the people.

He started with a service ticket—pump controller firmware acting "fluttery" in the Plumber's Closet. A junior tech from Power showed, badge clipped to his belt like a handle. Johnny fixed the "flutter" with a wipe and a wink, then borrowed thirty seconds of badge-and-terminal time to stage a diagnostic image on the shop machine. No admin, no writes—just a signed maintenance build that logged everything the controller saw to a buffer Johnny could read later.

Next came hardware. In a blind corner of a manifold cabinet he slid in a thumb-length shim—inline on the PLC bus, one-way mirror only. It timestamped traffic from cargo handling and external ops without touching a single byte. *Read-only or prison.* He stuck to read-only.

The software pivot was the riskiest. Engineering trend servers weren't air-gapped; they ingested copies of half the ship's life for convenience—temperatures, valve cycles, even cut-down nav telemetry for performance plots. Johnny used his "diagnostic" account to pull those trend exports, never the live systems. An audit heartbeat blinked red in the top corner of the console—ninety seconds before someone asked a question. He killed the session, walked the corridor twice, and came back as if the first man had been someone else.

Back in his sanctum he let the stolen buffers breathe. Long-range scanner echoes, trimmed for engineering, still kept enough truth: spikes that matched ejection windows, tug transponders that woke and slept at the same minutes, corridor sweeps that always "coincided" with a quiet deck. He mapped the pings by hand—dots, lines, arcs—until the Belt looked like a spider had built herself a freight line.

He cross-checked with what he could reach without tripping alarms: waste-handling weigh slips, galley delivery scrips, a few “misplaced” maintenance chits. The numbers grinned back. Product out, money in, records that smiled in public and screamed in private.

Johnny let out a breath he didn’t know he’d been holding. “Farragut,” he said to the dim room, “this has you and your boss Phoss written all over it.” In seconds his findings were bundled into an encrypted, condensed file. Two quick transmissions, and it was done. He checked the logs on his ghost account and saw the ACK confirming Earthside receipt.

A soft chime answered from the bulkhead. Someone upstairs wanted to know what he had found. Maybe they had heard his footprints in their snow, maybe not. Either way, Johnny was ready.

In his mind, he could hear the satisfying sound of the bolt sliding home as he chambered a round.

16. The Coup

Farragut read in silence, studied Johnny's holo-model, then thumbed a hidden switch. "SKIF mode engaged," the computer said. Admiral Phoss appeared. White at the temples. Dark eyes that did not waste time. "What is it Farragut?"

Farragut rotated the camera to Johnny's packet. Color drained from Phoss' face, then came back hard. "Captain, are you looking to get us both dropped into a very deep hole? What are you thinking, showing this to anyone not on the list?"

"Admiral Phoss, meet my S2, Master Plumber John Andretti. This report is his."

Johnny cut in. "Before we continue, understand I have a dead-man switch on this data. It's already staged Earthside. If I stop doing what I'm doing, it drops to fifteen thousand places at once. News agencies, conspiracy theorist hubs, politicians, even the dark web."

"You put this together?" Phoss was focused on his display, ignoring Johnny's carefully prepared statement.

"Right now, I'm asking the questions Admiral."

Unaccustomed to a lack of deference, Phoss' eyebrows lifted nearly to his hairline.

"If I don't like what I hear, if I think you're lying to me, this goes public."

Phoss' color returned to his face and anger flashed in his eyes. "Andretti, you're starting to piss me off."

Johnny smiled. "Take a number Phoss. Now, tell me, why is the Army Corps of Engineers building a systemwide shooting range with Earth in the crosshairs. Pensions not fat enough? Or you want to run the whole show yourselves, with a gun to everyone's head? Plotting a coup Admiral?"

Phoss tensed for a millisecond and then he laughed aloud. "You thought it was a coup? Oh, thank God. You had begun to scare me." Phoss shook his head, his relief visible and unfeigned.

Watching Phoss react, Johnny decided that either the Admiral was a superb actor, or the coup theory was the wrong pipe.

"Captain, read him in on the Belts part of Belts and Suspenders. I'm informing the Consuls. Oh, and Andretti, I'm having you read in on this so you will stop wasting time on unrelated activities. Solve this murder or you'll spend the rest of your days scrubbing toilets on one of those little rocks highlighted in your model."

The line died. Farragut smiled, an expression more unsettling than his scowl. "That went better than expected."

Johnny frowned. "Read me in?"

"Here's what you're missing in your model." Farragut closed Johnny's display and a more robust one appeared in its place.

Thirty minutes later Johnny was shaking his head in disbelief. "So. There is a Thalyrian empire of gilled, water-breathing versions of humans. Said empire is called the Sanctum, with 'Sanctifier' soldiers that would love to own us. A fatal shipwreck and a lucky communications break put us in touch with the Sanctifier's nicer cousins, the rebellious Consortium, instead of serving us up to the bad guys. The oh-so-kind Consortium rigged the table for creation of the UER. Odyssey is a listening post and an exchange hub for weaponizing the Belt as part of an anti-Sanctifier pro-Consortium defensive net."

Farragut nodded. "Nailed it in thirty seconds."

Johnny scoffed. "This not-a-coup story stinks like a fish market. Pun intended. Number one, the Belt is a ring inside a sphere. It's a space-age Maginot Line. Number two, how do we know they are not arming us with us pea shooters while their cousins carry machine guns? Three, what are the odds we stumbled into a bunch of benevolent galactic altruists instead of their power-mad cousins?"

"Is that all?"

"That's enough for now." Johnny was sure there was more to Phoss' story than 'Suspenders,' but with no more than a hunch to go on, he had to put a pin in that wriggling fish.

Farragut nodded. "On your first point, you're right about spherical defense. That part is Suspenders. That's outside of your need to know. Phoss is working directly for the Consuls. Bypassing the chain of command. Keeping operational security extremely tight. This call added your name to a very short list, at the top of which are the Consuls. Not a coup."

"If you say so Skipper," Johnny agreed verbally, All the alarms going off in his head could have shaken the hull plates off the Odyssey. *I'm supposed to be laying low on the Odyssey. Suddenly the most powerful people in the solar system know my name. So much for not getting caught. Odds are, this ends badly for me.*

Farragut went on "As for your other points, you're not the only one who doesn't believe in coincidences."

"How does Ham fit into this?"

"That's what you need to figure out for us."

Johnny fingered Ham's vial of cloudy water in his pocket. He pulled it out and set it on the table before Farragut. "This was in Ham's hand when he died."

"A vial of test water?"

"That's what I thought, at first. When I found three more just like it in Ham's cabin, hidden away like Captain Kidd's treasure, I reconsidered. It inspired me to dig for a bit of treasure too. I reached out to a friend back on Earth."

"That didn't happen. All your outbound calls are blocked as part of my security lockdown. Your dead-man switch was a bluff too. We caught the data packet and spoofed the acknowledgement."

Johnny shrugged. *Two data packets, one for the Skipper to catch and the other to land the punch,* he thought. Aloud, "If you say so Skipper. Want to know what I learned from the calls I never made and didn't receive?"

Farragut scowled, swallowed half his drink and growled. "Go on."

"AguaLibre folks are spreading stories that the UER is working with water breathing aliens called Thalyrians, specifically a group calling themselves The Consortium. It seems these gill heads are trying to buy shower water from folks."

"Shower water?"

"Living water, they call it. Water that has been used to wash human bodies. Pretty crazy huh? Given the accuracy of the first part of the rumor, it could be a game of two-truths and a lie. Or, not."

"Why would Thalyrians want dirty water?"

"Only they know for sure, but rumor has it that our dirty water makes them trip the light fantastic, like a nose full of cocaine. This little vial of water," Johnny shook it, "It's nothing to us. To a Thalyrian, it's worth its weight in gold. If a Thalyrian killed Ham, this wouldn't have been left behind." Johnny caught Farragut's tell that he was holding aces. "But you knew about this already, didn't you?"

"Know is a strong word, Andretti. But, so far, it's the only explanation that makes sense."

"Truth? I know it from Ham's notebook. Now, you know."

Farragut leaned in. "Thalyrians in the mix make it even more important to control the narrative. The circle of knowledge about Ham stays tight."

Johnny nodded in agreement. "No leaks. Everyone gets the story that Ham is a cracked white pipe leaking toxic black sludge. Quarantine is keeping what Ham has out of our drinking water."

"If a Thalyrian didn't kill Ham, you're thinking this was AguaLibre?"

"It fits."

"You're not convinced," it was a statement, not a question.

Johnny smiled. "Thalyrian's didn't kill Ham. A human did that."

"Get me a name, Andretti," Farragut growled, "and proof."

Names are easy, Johnny thought. *Proof gets people killed.*

17. Bay 16 Breach

Ship's night again. The Odyssey dimmed her lights like a guilty woman lowering her eyes. Johnny didn't trust her silences. He'd learned in too many back rooms that quiet wasn't peace, it was cover.

He took the crawlspace route behind Hydro, toolbox on his hip, boots set to whisper. The ducts here weren't on any tourist map. Half the crew didn't even know the passage existed. Johnny knew it because he made it his business to know. That was the difference between plumbing and killing: in one you traced the lines for leaks, in the other you traced the lines for lies. Both led to the same place eventually.

Getting caught here won't be a slap on the wrist. It'll be a quiet, and very fatal accident.

The crawl narrowed, ribbed steel pressing his shoulders, phantom lines, one black, one gray slid by his ear and plunged down a gap barely big enough for a rat before they bent their course in the same direction he was crawling. He dragged himself forward until he found a viewing port. Dinner-plate wide, rim smeared gray where someone had painted quick. He tried the latch. It didn't budge. Someone had welded it shut from the inside and smeared paint over the glass. Johnny smiled without humor. A man welded his windows when he had something to hide.

He crabbed farther down, feeling the vibration shift under his palms. The hum here was wrong—not the steady heartbeat of pumps, but a low growl with weight behind it. He found another port, this one overlooked by the welders. Paint scuffed but latch clean. He thumbed it open a crack. Cold air licked his face, damp with the tang of ice. With the care of a brain surgeon, he scraped a small patch off the haphazardly applied paint and then eased the port shut again.

Through the slot, Bay 16 lay sprawled beneath him like a crime scene waiting for discovery. Gantries hung over a cradle. Inside the cradle sat a pale sphere the size of a house, sweating in the light. Vapor curled off its skin and dripped into floor drains that gurgled too politely. Two figures in insulated suits mopped the runoff. A third stood at a console. Johnny zoomed the wrist lens and caught the log header: EJECTION WINDOW – 04:13.

The sphere looked alive in the half-light, breathing cold. Johnny's teeth ached just watching it. The Marines circling the ice were spraying it down. Adding mass. Johnny traced the hoses to the wall. He almost choked in amazement. The hoses were coming off gray lines. Phantom gray lines staring right at him.

Voices bled through an intercom: clipped, professional, never loud. He caught fragments—"sample integrity," "optimal organics threshold," "no chemical contamination," and one word that settled in his bones: "consignment."

Consignment meant commerce. Someone was selling the family silver.

A light beam swept the gantry, white-hot across the port. Johnny killed his wrist screen, pressed back into shadow, heart thudding in rhythm with the pumps. A boot rang magnetic against steel above him—clack, pause, clack. The step lingered, close enough he could imagine the breath inside the helmet. Then it moved on.

Johnny let out a breath, slow. He slid the lens back up, risked three stills: one of the tether drum readouts, one of a crate labeled ICE HOLD—AFT with a tidy consignment code, and one of the console clock ticking down to ejection.

Johnny was startled by the sound of heavy machinery. He glanced into the bay. The Marines had donned pressure suits and were tethered. Reflexively, Johnny pulled up the flexible helmet on his own pressure suit and sealed up. His gauge showed he had just fifteen minutes of air.

He turned his attention back to the Marines and their overgrown gray ice-cube.

They scrambled over the orb and drove in anchor loops, like outsized pitons a mountain climber might use, at several points with ruthless efficiency. Then they retreated. A mechanical arm reached into the bay from somewhere behind Johnny's field of view. From outside the Odyssey. Self-guided cables snaked out from the arm and fastened themselves to the anchors and then pulled taut. With a snap and crack of breaking ice, the orb of gray ice lifted off the floor mount and glided away, presumably into space.

Moments later, a roughhewn block of blue-green ice glided into the space where the orb had rested. Arm and cables retreated and Johnny heard the noise of machinery again. This time, he recognized the hiss of air as the chamber was repressurized. The Marines slid their faceplates back and attached vacuum hoses with red hot heads onto the rock of ice. In seconds water was flowing through the hoses and into a water purifier, bolted to the wall and disguised as a water transfer cabinet. Johnny stared at another phantom, black pipe emerging from the cabinet flowing into the complex web of clean water storage all over the Odyssey.

No wonder the water purification system is running so well. Johnny mused silently. It's mostly handling clean water while the real gray water is being jettisoned. Consigned, he corrected himself. Gray lines feed the ice. Black lines drink the melt, and bring the extra cold.

Johnny slid back his own hood and made a note in his official log, "Inspection complete. No anomalies."

Johnny pulled up the log on the tug-cam, a classified external video feed located at the 'far' end of the cigar. The end opposite the landing bay. Two unmanned exterior maintenance drones, their mechanical arms extended behind them, dragged the orb of frozen gray water aft and let it slide to the end of its tether into the void. Joining five other similar orbs dangling there.

The winking out of stars caught Johnny's attention. A shape that blocked out the stars and reflected no light seemed to slink up behind the Odyssey, growing larger as it approached. For a brief interval of less than a minute an eye-hurting deep blue light opened like a mouth in the starless void and it swallowed the half dozen balls of frozen gray water. The blue light went out and the darkness slid away, releasing more of the stars it had hidden with its approach until it was lost into the void. As it retreated the way it had come, the drones reeled in the tether lines onto spools anchored on the hull, then turned away to other duties.

Johnny glanced at his chronometer. It was now 04:18. Five minutes after the exchange; dirty water, gone; clean water, in the system. Johnny cemented a pin mic just below the lip of the porthole frame. No need for video. It would alert him every time this un-mapped hull portal opened and closed. Now, he would know whenever it cycled for transit.

In his personal log he noted, "Tethered sphere swap observed at ejection window 04:13. External drones. Unrecognizable receiver." *Everything's clean—like a kitchen that only ever cooks lies.* Johnny thought.

He crawled backward, slow and careful, the way you leave a room after you've killed someone and don't want to be noticed. When he dropped out of the crawlspace, Dunning was waiting in the corridor. Coveralls, no rank on display. Just her eyes, glinting in the gloom, steady as a firing line.

"Night jog?" Johnny asked. His voice was easy. His pulse wasn't.

"Exercise," she said. Not a bead of sweat on her. "You're not the first plumber I've found around here."

"Pipes go everywhere. Where pipes go, plumbers go."

"I don't know what you're up to Andretti, but I will find out. When I mentioned your snooping to Farragut, he told me to watch and report, only to him. But to not impede."

"Impede? That seems a bit vague. From what I have read, when Force Recon 'impedes,' there are casualties."

"His words, not mine. If it were my call, impede would be the *least* you could expect."

They held the stare a second too long. Then she stepped aside. No accusation. No small talk. Just a beat of silence that felt like a coin flipped in the dark.

Later, in his private log, a message appeared without sender stamp: *Don't come back the same way twice.*

Johnny didn't smile, though he wanted to. He filed the stills under a hydroponics maintenance header and made a note in his private book:

Bay 16 sweats.

Act IV Layers of Deception

Figure 4 On the Rocks

18. Update

Johnny sauntered across Farragut's office to stare out the porthole. A porthole was a rare luxury on Odyssey. Deliberately he pulled a cigarette from inside his coverall, followed by a lighter. He lit the cigarette and took a deep drag, feeling the nicotine hit his system and the smoke burn his lungs.

"I'm dropping my block on your comms, Andretti. It doesn't seem to be stopping you anyway."

"Don't. The shadow of your suspicion reinforces my cover."

"Then, what do you want?" Farragut asked without getting up from behind his desk.

Johnny laughed. "Not much Skipper. Just a little peace of mind, and a name."

"I don't have either for you."

"True that," Johnny nodded.

"Then what?"

Johnny took another deep drag before answering, watching the unwinking stars slide past as the station revolved on its axis. He turned away from the porthole and locked eyes with Farragut.

"I looked you up Skipper. You're the real deal."

"What do you mean?"

"You're a killer."

"I didn't kill the plumber."

Johnny studied Farragut for a moment. Despite the traces of gray in his hair, he was all hard planes. No fat. A sword personified in flesh and bone. Long, sharp edges that would cut through flesh and bone without slowing. "No. You didn't. But you could have. Honestly, of all the people on this barge most would have a hard time looking a man in the face and then killing him, up close and personal like that. But you could. You have."

"I did my duty."

"Duty?" Johnny chuckled. "Duty my ass. You like killing. I can see it in your eyes. And I can read it in your file, between the lines."

"You've overstepped your bounds with the personnel files."

"Did you think I would automatically disqualify you as a suspect because this is your boat?"

Farragut remained silent.

"What you did in the Philippines," Johnny shook his head. "That was epic, frightening, and amazingly inventive."

Farragut's voice was laced with threat. "That isn't in my file."

"Not in your military record." Johnny conceded. "This isn't my first murder Skipper. My hobbies, and my work, have forced me to learn a wide variety of things. Seeing info locks and slipping through them are just a part of what I bring to the table."

"That seems like an odd skill set for a plumber."

"That depends entirely on the sort of leaks a plumber is fixing."

Farragut's eyebrows came together in puzzlement. "What are you saying?"

Johnny rechecked the settings on his wrist communicator before answering. "Before I tell you what I mean, I want you to know that I've temporarily looped all recording and surveillance devices in this room. What I'm about to tell you will leave less evidence than a whisp of water vapor in a tornado. What's more, repeating what I say will get you dead."

Farragut rose to his feet, his fingertips resting on his desktop. His shoulders hunched, his knees bent, ready to spring. "I don't respond well to threats," he snarled.

"I know. No threat. A promise. You see, I'm a killer too."

Farragut shifted his weight slightly toward his heels.

"The difference between us? I kill for money, and usually only one person at a time. I admit, your body count is much higher than mine, but I never used laser-guided bombs dropped from 30,000 feet to take out any of my targets. About half of mine I used my bare hands."

"Why tell me this?"

"Skipper, you need to know what I am so when I bring you Ham's killer you'll take me seriously."

"How does you telling me this achieve that?"

"It might not," Johnny acknowledged. "But it's the best way I could think of. Your inquiries with the RBI all came up dry. If anyone in the government had an accurate file on me, I would be dead or in prison."

"How do I know you're telling me straight?" Farragut's inquiries with the Republic Bureau of Investigation had given him no new information. As far as the RBI was concerned, Johnny was a Master Plumber, with his own company and a reputation that got him exclusive, highly paid, plumbing jobs all over the world. No one had ever tied him to anything more sinister than a speeding ticket.

"Look me in the eyes Skipper." Johnny stepped up to Farragut's desk leaned in so that mere inches separated their faces. "I'm a professional killer. I've been a hitman for the

Mob since I was fifteen.[11] I've dropped bodies all over the world. Never been a suspect."

"You don't look like a mobster, or a hit man,"

"Exactly. I blend in and don't leave evidence: electronic, physical, or forensic. I learned all about that, so that I could be the best at what I do. What's the old saying, it takes a thief to catch a thief? I'm a killer; that's why I'll catch your killer."

"If being a killer were enough, I've got a ship full of killers, as you already mentioned."

"True, Skipper. It's a lot, but not enough for this job. I'm not *just* a triggerman. I find leaks, operational, informational, systemic leaks, and stop them. Me being a plumber was an inside joke in the family."

"Give me one piece of evidence to corroborate your 'ambitious' back story."

"Proof gets people killed, Skipper," he locked eyes with Farragut for a long moment. Then nodded slightly.

"Seven years ago, as a special request, a favor, I took the only government job I've ever done. Remember the charismatic Consul-Designate Arturo Mendez?"

"I vaguely remember him. He made a lot of noise sympathetic to AguaLibre." Farragut demurred.

"Some say he was the founder."

"I wouldn't know."

"You and Phoss were tasked with running 'Red Team' scenarios focused on taking him out."

---

[11] See Black File BF-U-008 Blood and Ice Johnny A. Union Access Required

"How would you know that?"

"We covered that ground when we discussed your fun in the Philippines, remember?"

Farragut glared at Johnny, "The exercise was done to harden his security. We were stood down when Mendez died in a gas explosion."

"Amazingly bad luck, or good luck, depending on your perspective. Don't you think?"

"It wasn't good luck for him."

"It was for the UER, as well as you and Phoss."

"How so?"

"You never had to go live on any of your Red Team scenarios, and the UER never had to cover up, or find scapegoats for, an assassination."[12]

"His death was an accident."

"He, and his two closest aides, entered the building through a secure, secret passage to the reception hall. The three of them stopped in a narrow hallway to have a private conversation with a fourth person. His guards closed the doors at either end of the hallway to give them privacy."

"There was nothing in the papers about any fourth person."

"True," Johnny acknowledged. "But you and I both had orders to punch that guy's ticket anytime and anywhere we

---

[12] See Black Files: BF-U-002 Gaslight Near Miss. Union Access

found him. Pierre Etain was a suspected Thalyrian agent and a known AguaLibre terrorist. I didn't find out about the Thalyrian part of his background until recently. Still, I got a bonus for dropping him in the accident."

"So, how did you do it?"

"Two weeks before the event, I was called in to fix a plumbing problem. The leak was a sewer pipe accessible through a small maintenance closet adjoining that little hallway. Running alongside the sewer pipe was a small gas line. I rigged the gas line to spring a leak on command. When they approached the hallway, the leak opened. They stopped in the closed off hallway, unaware of the gas wrapping around their knees from the ruptured a gas line."

"Mendez loved his nicotine. Any excuse to smoke in private and he would light up." Farragut nodded. "All four were killed instantly; their bodies pulped by the enclosed blast wave, while only two of the security team were injured."

Farragut looked into Johnny's eyes, the presence and identity of the fourth man wasn't mentioned in any unclassified report. After a long moment, Farragut nodded. "I believe you."

"Good. Because this is more of a … What did Phoss call it?" Johnny's fingers snapped. "A read-in than either of my ex-wives ever got in nine years of marital bliss."

"You were married twelve years," Farragut recalled from his research.

"True, but only nine were blissful," Johnny shot back. Now, I need to know what's going on in Bay Sixteen?"

Farragut's eyes sparked, but his face went blank. "I don't see how that relates to the murder."

"I don't know for sure that it does. However, that's the biggest secret on this barge, and could be why Ham was killed."

"Why would Ham get killed over Bay Sixteen?"

"Skipper, as I see it, there are four ways you own a ship without wearing your stripes: One, control the supply; what moves and when. For Odyssey water's the critical commodity. Weapons are second. Two, control the chokepoints; bays, ejection windows, corridors, viewports. Three, control the records; official logs smile while private logs keep score. Four, control the story; who's 'read in,' which drills run, who the paperwork blesses when it goes sideways. Someone in Bay Sixteen owns the valves, the doors, the ledgers, and the rumor mill. And, the dots are lining up on Ham's old pal Lieutenant Dunning."

The hardening line of Farragut's mouth let Johnny know his spread of torpedoes had all hit their marks. Farragut's ship was taking on water and he needed to take evasive maneuvers. "What's that got to do with Ham?"

"Reviewing his movements has been challenging. Bay Sixteen is a black hole for ordinary video monitoring. Still, from Ham's notes and watching him fall into and out of that black hole, I can see that he had an unhealthy fascination with all things related to Bay Sixteen. Outside of the black hole,

Ham and Dunning were constantly bumping into one another."

"If you crawl over the same pipes he did won't you come down with the same health problem?"

"It's a risk," Johnny admitted. "But, there's a key difference between Ham and me."

"Which is?"

"I'm working for you."

"And Ham?"

"If I'm right. Ham wasn't just a plumber. He was a Thalryian spy."

"Which side?"

"I'm not sure," *And not sure it matters. If Ham was spying, odds were good he hadn't been spying for the same side I think I'm on.*

19. Rao

Johnny's next maintenance call went right into Bay 16.

"Rao. That your name?" Johnny asked as he visually inspected the pipes.

"Yep. Rafael Vinicius Iyer Duarte Raoni. My father is Brazilian. My Mother was an Indian engineer working in Sao Paulo. In India Rao means lord." Rao thumped his chest proudly. He had the look of two worlds welded together; carioca swagger and eyes that were constantly probing for an angle. He flashed a cocky grin and tapped his two chevrons: "Spec-Three. Fluids."

"So, you're here to see if I know what I'm doing?"

Rao laughed. "No man. This is a Secure space. I have clearance and you don't. I'm here to make sure you don't mess with anything classified."

"Copy. You're the hall monitor." Johnny spotted the symptoms of a cracked pipe joint. As he talked, he drew out his tools and carried out the repair, almost on autopilot. "So, if I stick my nose where I shouldn't you gonna stop me?"

"Damn straight," Rao replied confidently.

"You?"

"Hell yes. I've been in combat. I'm trained in hand-to-hand." Rao pointed to another patch on his uniform, "I got this one for service in the Pacific. Things got real hot there and I held my own. Also, I was born in the back streets of Rio. In those slums, if you're not a hustler, or a muscler, you're somebody's honey-pot."

Johnny put down his kit and turned to Rao. "Let's do an experiment. You up for that Specialist Rao? Let's pretend I'm trying to do something I shouldn't. Hit me."

"I don't want to hurt you, old man."

Johnny beckoned with one hand, the other hanging at his side. "Show me if you were a muscler in Rio. Give it a shot."

"Nah," Rao turned away and then suddenly tried a roundhouse he'd been saving for a smaller man.

Johnny slid half a step, let the kick sail through dead air, palmed Rao's shoulder and set him gently into a bulkhead. "Careful," Johnny said. "Valves bruise."

Two very large Marines stepped into the compartment. Both were wearing duty belts and sidearms. Their oddly angled caps seemed welded to their nearly shaved scalps. They focused their attention on Johnny, while speaking only to Rao. "We heard a noise. Is there a problem here Specialist?"

Rao sprang up onto his feet, glaring at Johnny. "No worries, guys. I just lost my balance."

"He was showing me some of the moves he used in combat." Johnny offered.

The two Marines looked back and forth between Johnny and Rao. Disdain for both bled from their eyes. "You done here," the Marine read Johnny's name tag. "Andretti?"

Johnny nodded. "Here, yes, but you see that pipe there?" he pointed to the pipe coming out of the joint he had just repaired. "That one goes into the adjoining compartment. Its pressure reading is too low. I suspect it may be leaking and I need to run it down."

The Marines looked at one another. One nodded and left the room. The other remained, blocking the door. "Give us a minute Mister Andretti. Lieutenant Dunning told us to make sure you were able to get your work done. However, she also told us to make sure that any classified materials or equipment should be kept out of your sight."

"I understand. Are Lance Corporals Hess and Arnold cleared for everything in that room?"

"Yes sir. All the Marines here are cleared."

Johnny pulled up his wrist unit and raised Hess and Arnold on it. "What's up Johnny?"

"I need you two in Bay Sixteen right away. Following a potential leak and the Marines here are telling me the room I need to check has classified stuff. I need you two to look where I can't."

"On our way."

The Marine blocking the door relaxed slightly. "I wondered where those two had gotten off to."

"Lieutenant Dunning assigned them to help me while my Journeyman is WIA."

"Ham's still sick?" Rao asked. To Johnny's ears, Rao's voice carried a note of concern, and a symphony of speculation over potential opportunity.

"Quarantined. He's in tough shape. I've picked up *all* his work." As he emphasized the word 'all' he gave Rao a meaningful look. "His *whole* book of business is in my hands now."

Rao shifted his weight nervously from foot to foot. His anger and embarrassment giving way to trepidation.

The other Marine returned. "You're all clear now. Except, don't touch any equipment that is covered."

"Can Hess or Arnold touch it for me?"

"Sure, but you can't look inside, or even at the consoles unless they are covered."

Johnny smiled amiably. "I guess they'll just have to be my eyes and hands. We'll see how well I've trained them."

Three sets of boots came tramping down the passageway. The two Marines snapped to attention and saluted as Lieutenant Dunning entered the room. Hess and Arnold on her heels. Rao snapped to attention as well.

"As you were," she told Johnny's guards. "What are you up to Andretti? Since when do you roam around Bay Sixteen?"

"L-T," Johnny used the too familiar nickname for any Lieutenant. He was pleased to see one corner of her mouth turn down slightly in displeasure. To Johnny that corner of her mouth was the home of her most noticeable tells "So good to see you again. I see you found the knights errant you loaned me. Thank you so much for escorting them."

"Andretti, I don't like repeating myself. I asked a question. Answer now, or I'll have these two kick your ass all they from here to the hangar."

Johnny shrugged. "Been a long time since I had that much fun." He paused. Just as her mouth turned down again, he continued. "But I really don't have time for a jam session with your band right now. I'm tracking a leak and it's brought me here. I just fixed that faulty joint there, but the line is still reading too low and it goes right through this bulkhead into the next compartment."

Dunning looked at Rao, who shrugged in response. The corner of her mouth turned up slightly.

"Specialist Rao. Perhaps Guardian boot camp failed to teach you proper military etiquette, or you've forgotten it. I don't really care which. If you ever shrug at me again instead of giving me a response appropriate to my rank, after you're discharged from the med bay you'll spend six months cleaning grease traps in the galley. Is that clear?"

Rao and Dunning were less than a foot from one another at this point. Eyes locked and ignoring everyone else in the room. Although the two were almost interchangeable from a build and coloration standpoint, Johnny could see that where Dunning was a barracuda, Rao was soft and eel-slippery, but weak. *Weak pipes cut you when they break*, Johnny thought to himself.

Rao snapped to attention and real fear showed in his eyes. "Yes sir. I saw the plumber fix the joint as he stated. The readings he took showed the same low pressure in the line as he noted previously, sir."

Satisfied, Dunning eyed the two guards. "Have you secured the next compartment?"

"Yes sir."

"Good. Andretti, carry on. Rao, Hess, and Arnold, help as needed." She turned and left. The chorus of "Aye, aye, sir," echoing down the passageway behind her.

In the next room Johnny traced the water line from the bulkhead into the back of a console that the Marines had covered up. Finding the output water line Johnny tested both. He waved Rao, Hess, and Arnold over and repeated his test, making sure all three could see the readings.

"What do you see, and what does it tell you?"

Arnold spoke first, "higher pressure going in, lower coming out. Most likely a leak in there."

"Most likely." Johnny agreed. He looked expectantly at the three young men. "Well, what are you waiting for? I'm not authorized to open that box. So, it's on you three to get in there and fix it. I'll check the other lines while you open her up. Then, I'll talk you through the repairs, if you need it."

Just as promised, Johnny checked the rest of the lines in the room and found two more with suspicious readings. By the time all three leaks had been eliminated Rao, Hess, and Arnold all knew the basics of repairing water leaks and cleaning up, Johnny having also talked them through collecting all the leaked water from inside the machines. Johnny ran a quick system diagnostic.

He nodded. "Looks like you boys caught the last of the leaks for now. Never fear though. On a cruise ship like this, built by the lowest bidder, you can bet tomorrow we'll have more to fix."

"Hess, Arnold, call it a day." Johnny turned to Rao. "Specialist Rao, walk me out of Bay Sixteen." He turned and started back toward the main entrance to the bay. Once they were out of earshot of anyone else Johnny spoke quietly, without looking at Rao as they walked.

"I've reviewed Ham's books and discussed it with him. You're light."

"Like Hell you have. Nobody in Sick Bay would let me near Ham."

"Whatever Ham's got, I've already been exposed. Only Wu and I see him. Your next delivery needs to make up the gap, plus twenty percent for the vig."

Rao's mouth fell open and he stopped in his tracks. Johnny kept walking. Rao quick-stepped and caught up with him. "You're joking right? Ham never charged interest. He knows I'm good for it."

"Ham's an amateur. I came up in Philly. Been dealing with punks like you all my life. You don't pay? If I'm feeling generous you get a limp for the rest of your life. If not, I'll toss your thieving carcass out an airlock."

"You threatening me, old man?"

"I don't threaten, Rao. Threats are IOUs for men without the funds. I always pay cash." Without looking or breaking stride Johnny's left hand shot out, punching Rao in the side of his head.

Rao ricochetted off the bulkhead. As he staggered back Johnny caught him by the back of his pants and lifted him slightly into the air with one hand. To a casual observer it looked as though Johnny had kept Rao from falling after the young man had managed to collide with the wall.

"Now, you've pissed me off. Deal's changed. The vig is now thirty percent. Pay the whole freight today, by twenty-one hundred hours, or buy yourself some crutches because you are gonna have a knee that will pain you every-time the weather changes." Johnny twisted the waist of the pants and lifted Rao onto his tiptoes. "Clear?"

Rao opened his mouth to protest.

"You wanna go fifty?" Johnny warned. "Or maybe you think you can take me?" Johnny smiled and made Rao appear to stagger a little with his grip on Rao's pants.

"Twenty-one hundred hours. One hundred thirty percent. Where?"

"I'll let you know where. Don't be late."

Five minutes before 9 pm ship's time, 2100 hours, Rao's communicator buzzed. He read the message from Johnny. His eyebrows raised and then, he set off at a brisk pace, a large Marine in civilian clothes trailing behind him.

Promptly at 2100 hours Rao stepped into the ship's firing range. Johnny was standing there in the semidarkness talking with Lieutenant Dunning. A half dozen Marines were on the firing line. The 'buzz' and 'thump' of their shoulder fired rail guns made a quiet staccato rhythm.

"Rao," Johnny greeted the Brazilian. "Here to square your bets with me?"

"Andretti," Dunning interrupted sharply. "Gambling is forbidden on the Odyssey."

"Do you want to bet that there are plenty of friendly wagers going on all the time?"

"Is that the sort of wagers we're talking here?"

Johnny laughed. "With Ham out of commission, do you really think I have time to run a gambling ring?"

"I'm guessing if anyone could manage it Andretti it would be you."

"Where I grew up, that'd be a compliment."

"Not." Dunning turned to the Marine trailing Rao. "Corporal Scarpo, is there something you need here?"

"No sir. Just kicking it with Rao. He promised some fun."

Johnny studied Scarpo. Medium height, solidly built, and moved with the natural grace of a hunting cat. The gleam in Scarpo's eye let Johnny know this was a man who enjoyed hurting and killing. The Yin to Rao's Yang.

In his head Johnny pulled up Scarpo's file. Scout Sniper. A military assassin. Most of his missions were redacted. Surgical hits on key military targets and some black ops for intelligence agencies. Early in his investigation Johnny had considered Scarpo a suspect, but his work with spies ruled him out. The fact that Rao had invited Scarpo to their meeting told Johnny that Rao was willing to kill over the water business.

"Corporal Scarpo," Johnny turned to the Marine, "what's your military specialty?"

Scarpo smiled, his eyes cold. "Killing."

Johnny laughed. "That's what I hear from all these Force Recon Marines. You one of them?"

Scarpo leaned back slightly, just a small change in his stance. He tapped his chest. "Scout Sniper."

Johnny nodded respectfully. He glanced at Dunning. "The Lieutenant here was about to show me how to shoot this new rifle. Are you familiar with it?" Dunning helpfully held up the rifle she and Johnny had been discussing.

Scarpo nodded. "I fired some early prototypes. Told them how to make it better."

"Wanna make sure this is sighted properly before I try it out?"

Scarpo shrugged. "Sure. You okay with that Lieutenant?"

Dunning, face expressionless, laid the rifle on the firing bench and stepped away, giving Scarpo access to the rifle.

Scarpo sauntered to the firing bench. With practiced ease he inspected the weapon, loaded it and aimed it downrange. A slight hum, followed by one mild thump. He set the rifle down and looked up at the overhead video feed of his target, 1500 meters downrange. The man shaped silhouette had a single hole in the center of the forehead.

"It's good." He stepped away from the bench.

"Thanks. Lieutenant, may I try it now?" Johnny asked.

Dunning nodded.

Johnny picked up the rifle, sighted, and fired. A hole appeared in the kneecap of the target. The Marines stifled chuckles and Rao laughed aloud.

"Crap. I must have jerked that." Johnny mumbled in evident embarrassment. "Of course, that would leave a guy with a knee that will predict the weather for the rest of his life. Wouldn't it Rao?" Rao stopped laughing.

Johnny fired again. This time a hole appeared squarely in the crotch of the target. "Musta jerked it again."

"Man or woman," Dunning said, "that's gonna hurt." The men chuckled while shifting from foot to foot in sympathetic discomfort.

"One more try," Johnny offered.

Scarpo didn't look at the target. He watched Johnny's hands, his breathing, his posture.

The plumber squeezed off a third round. Hum. Thump. The computer highlighted Scarpo's headshot.

"Musta missed the whole thing," Johnny grumbled. Rao and the Marines laughed.

"Nope," Scarpo offered in a low voice. "Your third went right through my shot. The computer verified it. Twice."

Silence.

Johnny shuffled his feet and set the rifle down with a shrug. "Lucky shot," he mumbled. Then stepped back from the bench. Appearing to recover from his slouch of embarrassment he turned to Rao. "Now, about that money you owe?"

Rao gawked at the displayed target for a moment. Johnny watched as his eyes travelled from the improbable shot in the forehead to the crotch and the knee. Rao's mouth closed and he gulped hard. He handed Johnny a credit SIM card; common practice aboard ship. It was the equivalent of cash that anyone could use.

"It's all there," Rao nearly whispered, his eyes not leaving the illuminated target. He stepped back a half step.

Scarpo stepped forward. "That was a hell of a shot. Especially for an amateur."

Johnny smiled, his own eyes cold. "Professionals built the Titanic. An amateur built the Ark."

Dunning coughed to cover a bark of laughter.

Johnny could see from the mild confusion in Scarpo's eyes that the reference was lost on him. "Read a book," Johnny advised.

Scarpo smiled tightly at Johnny. "You're a funny guy. Fingers crossed your luck doesn't run out."

Johnny shrugged. He pivoted to Dunning, dismissing Scarpo with the move. "I'd really like to run something past you Dunning. It's a bit late tonight, but can you carve out some time for me. There's something I wanna get your take on."

"I've got a full day tomorrow. Is it urgent, or can it wait until the day after?"

"That's soon enough. Neither of us is going anywhere. I'll send you the location and time." Johnny started to turn away, then he turned back. "Thanks again for showing me that new Mark 92 slug thrower. With a DU round I'm betting that could knock a hole in a ship at five clicks."

"What do you know about depleted uranium rounds?" Scarpo interrupted.

Johnny turned to face the Marine again. "Only what I read. And that's enough to know that we wouldn't even want to test fire one of those in here. Maybe we can try that one day on the external range?" He looked hopefully at Dunning.

She shook her head. "Not a chance." Dunning looked at Johnny's face and realized she had just confirmed the presence of DU rounds for the station's guns. She verbally lurched forward. "If we were ever to have any of those rounds here it would only be for use on larger meteors or rogue asteroids."

"Of course, Lieutenant," Johnny interrupted her sudden verbal misstep while making a mental note to check if DU rounds being clandestinely shipped into the Belt. "I was just joking around."

"Sure. A joke," Scarpo chuckled. "C'mon Rao. Where's that bit of fun you promised me?" Scarpo turned away with Rao in tow.

Walking away Scarpo called out over his shoulder, "you're a funny guy Andretti. I hope you keep that sense of humor. Right up until they scrape you off a bulkhead."

20. Booze and Babes

"Johnny," Rao tried to sound pleased when he picked up the plumber's call.

"Plumbers Closet. Now. Alone," was all Johnny offered before he cut the link.

Moments later Johnny could see Rao approaching the door to the closet. At the same time, Johnny could see Scarpo running laps around the hangar deck with a platoon of Marines.

Johnny opened the door before Rao could knock. The sharp tang of harsh chemicals rolled out the door and punched Rao in the nose. He sneezed and shook his head. "I hope Ham gets back on his feet soon. He never let it smell this bad in here."

"Spilled sludge sample. Chemicals smell better than sludge." Johnny offered.

The single lamp in the tight space cast the metal shelves into hard relief; two dented cups sat on a crate turned table, folding chairs positioned off one corner. Silently Johnny pointed to a chair and Rao sat. He pushed one of the cups at Rao. "Drink," he ordered.

Rao lifted his cup and swallowed; smiling as if it's the best thing he has tasted in weeks. "Earth booze is a luxury up here. This keeps the crew happy."

"People are paying Kitchen Weasel for this?"

"It's a sin they can afford. This and the jee-new." Rao laughed. His laugh was like oil dribbling through a machine, more of a gurgle than a laugh. "The two oldest pleasures. Even under the watchful eye of old Wild Bill some manage to ply the oldest profession to supplement their day jobs. Vice always dances just out of official lines of sight. Right?"

"You running prostitutes and water, Rao?"

"Booze and booty? That'd be a winning hand. Unfortunately, no. Scarpo hogs the jee-new action for himself." Rao shrugged. "The customer pays the jee-new, or he makes the customer pay with pain as their vig. I think he gets off on hurting folks. Do you?"

"Do I think Scarpo likes to hurt folks? Yes. Ham didn't mention running hookers. He and Scarpo in that together?"

"Scarpo don't play well with others. He and Ham didn't mingle. Do you like to hurt people, just like Scarpo?"

Johnny let a slight smile curl one corner of his mouth. Enough to make Rao think that he was saying, 'yes.' Aloud "Ham's out sick. His books aren't. Your numbers still aren't right."

Rao's smile folded. "Not right? You just don't understand how the cycles run—"

Johnny moved before the lie warmed the air, snapping Rao's wrist toward the deck until cartilage creaked. Rao came off his chair and onto his knees, whimpering in pain.

Johnny's grip didn't falter. He sounded as calm as if discussing a clogged valve. "Don't play games with me Rao. I have the real readings on the meters. You take ten and pay for eight, but you're sloppy. I won't tolerate you cheating me, or Ham. Doc says Ham might not make it. Did you slip something to Ham? Did you put him in the Med Bay? Or, do you know who did?"

Rao hissed. "I gave him his cut—"

Johnny flexed Rao's wrist another degree. It was a controlled movement, professional, a fraction too far and things tear. He leaned in, his face inches from Rao's. "Look me in the eye Rao."

Rao's eyes were shut, watering in pain. Johnny applied more pressure and Rao yelped and opened his eyes.

Rao's eyes cast wildly around the tiny room, begging for escape before they locked on Johnny. "No, Andretti, I had nothing to do with Ham getting sick. Why would I? He's been laying the golden eggs for me."

"You make this right—every liter, every transfer—or you disappear. No prints. No trail. That's not a promise. That's a guarantee." Rao's Adams Apple bobbed as he tried to swallow. His head bobbed.

Johnny bent Rao's wrist a littler further, the joints were ready to pop, ligaments stretching to their utmost limits. "I need to hear you say it."

"I'm sorry Andretti," Rao whimpered, looking up a Johnny. "I'll make it right. It won't happen again."

He released Rao's hand and leaned back in his chair. Rao clambered unsteadily to his feet.

"I cut you some slack on your screwups. With Ham taking ill so sudden, I knew there might be a little friction. Now, you knew the score, I figure you'll fly right." Johnny's tone was friendly, conciliatory. "Did I read you right Rao?"

Rao nodded.

"No more friction Rao. This was your last warning. Make everything right by oh-eight-hundred tomorrow." The last had the tonality of an executioner's axe hitting bone.

"I'll fix it," Rao almost whispered meekly. But his hands were fists, knuckles white. To Johnny, the apology sounded thin. In the silence Johnny heard the furnace-quiet of a man who no longer sees options but a single, bright line.

Johnny pulled Rao around by the front of his shirt and shoved him toward the hatch. "Out," he said simply. "And don't forget to use a cold pack. Your wrist will swell if you don't."

Rao stumbled into the corridor and down the passageway. When he reached the corner he looked back at the closed hatch of the Plumber's Closet. His eyes glinted and his lips hardened into a snarl. "You may think you got it all going your way old man. But what comes your way next, you won't see coming." If the microphones Lafferty installed hadn't been the best quality, Johnny would never have heard Rao's muttered threat, but he could read it plainly behind the mask Rao tried to push over it.

Johnny waited until the echo of Rao's boots died down before he keyed the hatch shut. He listened to the low hum of the ship's circulators and the quiet hiss of his own breath as the adrenaline bled out of him, leaving a metallic taste in his mouth.

He sat, staring at the dented cups still on the crate. They smelled faintly of yeast and rotting food — the rotgut brew cooked up in the galley by the pot scrubbing sailor, Kitchen Weasel.

Rao's whining rang through his head. *Rao doesn't know Ham's dead.*

Scarpo could have done it, but there was no evidence that his and Ham's rackets had overlapped.

Johnny's own drink cup remained untouched, reflecting the overhead light in a perfect oval. *Booze and water theft were two halves of the same scam, with the prostitution thrown in for grins and giggles,* he thought. *Rao lying and skimming; Ham bleeding and dying, and somebody pulling strings through the pipes.*

Johnny exhaled slowly, knuckles whitening against his knees. *A little vice like booze and babes, or even water theft, doesn't justify murder. There's a racket here I can't see yet, one worth killing for — and I don't plan to be a fatality.*

He needed answers. And he knew just where to look.

Lieutenant Dunning had been too quick to offer him "assistants." She'd kept her mask steady — but her eyes had flickered when he mentioned Bay Sixteen. She'd come looking when he'd rerouted the cold-making gear destined for Bay 16. *Three points confirm a straight line,* Johnny remembered from his high-school geometry class.

Johnny rose, straightened his coveralls, and keyed off the lights. "Time to dance, Lieutenant."

He left the plumbers' closet behind and headed toward the Marine training deck — where Dunning's squad ran their morning hand-to-hand drills.

He didn't plan to spar.

He planned to *interrogate. The trick would be getting answers without blowing his carefully leaky reputation to hell.*

21. Punching Up

When he entered the Marine training space one of them stepped in front of him, blocking his way. "No leaky pipes for you to fix in here Plumber. This area's off limits to civilians."

Johnny tried to look a little intimidated. It wasn't a disguise he wore easily, or well. "I um. I'm here at the invitation of Lieutenant Dunning."

The Marine turned his head slightly to project his voice over his shoulder, never taking his eyes off Johnny. "L.T." he bellowed. "Someone here to see you."

Dunning looked up from across the mat where she was taping her hands. She did it the way a professional wraps a present — neat, deliberate, too much practice.

"No worries Sergeant," she called out, her voice reverberating through the training area. "The Plumber told me he wants to *practice* some hand-to-hand."

The Sergeant smiled and several Marines chuckled.

"Got it, Sir. I'll take care of it."

"No thanks," she called out. "This session's mine."

More Marines chuckled and started passing the word along. "The LT is going to deliver a can of whup-ass on a DF civvie."

"FAFO Plumber," the Sergeant stepped aside to let Johnny pass. "Any next of kin I should notify?"

Johnny glanced from the Sergeant to Dunning. "Just a friendly sparring session. Right? FAFO?"

"Fool around and find out, Plumber. Dunning's gonna put you in a hurt locker," the Sergeant laughed as he clarified.

Dunning called out, "What's the matter Andretti? Afraid of getting your ass kicked by a girl? Perhaps I misheard? I thought you asked to spar, not train?"

"Sparring is good, Dunning. But I've got forty pounds on you. That's a lot more kinetic energy than you can deliver."

She smiled. "That assumes you land a punch."

The gym smelled faintly of sweat and disinfectant — the universal perfume of people who were hammers instead of carpenters. Johnny rolled his shoulders as he stepped barefoot onto the padded deck. The half-gravity made everything feel both lighter and slower, a strange kind of dream. Dunning was already there, stretching, her Marine-issue tank clinging to muscles that were wiry but not bulky. She looked like a blade — not heavy, just sharp.

"You sure you want to do this, Plumber?" she asked. Her tone was teasing, but her eyes weren't.

"Gotta stay limber," Johnny said, pulling his jumpsuit down to his waist. "Never know when I'll have to wrestle a pipe… or a Marine. Can't keep patching pipes all the time without a little live fire, right?"

She smiled faintly, but it didn't reach her eyes. "That what you call it? Live fire?"

"Call it prevention," he said. "Stops the leaks before they start."

"Pipes and hoses don't fight back."

"Ever wrestle a broken line under pressure? It kicks, punches, bites, scratches, cuts, and says the most obscene things about your mother. How much worse can a Marine be?"

"Big talk for a civilian."

He grinned. "Big words for a junior officer."

They circled. Dunning came in fast — a jab-cross-hook combo that was too clean to be casual. Johnny blocked the first two, let the hook graze his shoulder, and smiled like it hadn't hurt.

"Holding back?" he asked.

"Just warming up."

He moved in close, tied her up in a clinch, one hand on her elbow, the other brushing the back of her neck. The move looked casual, but his voice was low, almost conversational. "Tell me something, Lieutenant — what was Ham doing down by Bay Sixteen the day before he … ended up in such bad shape?"

She froze a fraction too long before twisting free. "You questioning me, Plumber? Bay Sixteen is a restricted area."

"Just making conversation. I want to figure out what … took him off the board. Wouldn't want anyone else to suffer the same fate." He sidestepped her next kick and hooked her ankle midair, dumping her on her back. The impact thudded through the mat. She rolled up fast, furious.

"You think I had something to do with Ham's situation?"

Johnny shrugged. "I think you knew him better than you're letting on."

She feinted left, swung right. This time she landed clean across his ribs. He grunted — not from pain, but satisfaction. She was telling him more with her hits than her words. The punch was a warning.

"Ham talked too much," she snapped, breathing hard. "Maybe he opened his mouth at the wrong moment, got a mouth full of dirty water and caught that nasty bug."

Johnny pressed, stepping inside her reach. He swept her leg; she countered with a shoulder roll that brought them chest to chest. Their forearms locked. His voice dropped to a whisper.

"A Bay Sixteen bug?"

Her eyes flickered, just once. Confirmation. She slammed her forehead into his nose — a perfect Marine break move. He stumbled back, blood slicking his lip.

"Done dancing?" he asked, wiping his mouth. His tone was calm — too calm.

"Not until one of us quits."

Johnny stepped back in, faster than before. They traded blows — knee, elbow, counter — each hit landing harder than the last. Other Marines in the area, at first resentful of a civilian in their midst, began to watch the action more closely, uncertain if this was sparring or combat.

Johnny slipped behind her, arm snaking around her throat. Not enough to choke — enough to make her listen. "Who are you protecting, Lieutenant?"

Her fingers clawed at his wrist. "You're way out of your depth, plumber."

"Maybe. But I'm not the one sucking air right now."

He released her suddenly, and she spun away, gasping. For a long second they just stared — predator to predator, breathing in sync.

"You're good," she admitted, rubbing her neck.

"I'm thorough," he said. "It's a plumbing thing. Follow the leak, find the pressure point."

"And what do you think you just found?"

Johnny smiled faintly. "A blockage. Somewhere near Bay Sixteen."

Dunning's eyes narrowed. "Then you should probably watch what you say. Words carry into odd corners of this place." She moved in a whirling blur.

"Do they?" He caught her leg mid-kick, pivoted, and dumped her flat on her back. The mat bounced. She rolled, came up breathing hard. "That sounded like advice."

"Observation," she said, brushing a strand of hair back. "People who talk too much get themselves hurt."

"Or worse."

Her eyes flicked up — just for a second, just long enough to register surprise. A micro-expression. The kind that told him everything.

He gave her a grin that wasn't friendly. "You hit softer than I expected."

She lunged, fury covering fear. A blur of strikes — sharp, controlled, all muscle memory. Johnny caught her arm, spun her, pressed her into the mat. The fight went quiet except for their breathing.

"You're pretty good," she said through her teeth.

"The touch of death always gives the best lessons." He leaned down, his voice almost a whisper. "You really ought to tell command if you've seen anything unusual in your department. Missing tools. Foot traffic where it doesn't belong."

"I haven't seen anything," she said instantly — too fast, too clean.

He held her another second, long enough for her pulse to thud against his forearm. Then, he let go.

Dunning sat up, glare sharp enough to cut steel. "Next time, plumber, stick to pipes."

"Next time, Lieutenant," he said, wiping a smear of sweat and blood from his jaw, "try not to telegraph your moves."

She stood, expression smoothing back into composure, but her knuckles were white.

"I don't know what you think you're looking for," she said.

Johnny smiled. "Sure you do. You just don't know I know."

She froze, then laughed once, short and brittle. "You're swimming in dangerous surf."

"Maybe," Johnny said. "But I'm still floating. Can you say the same? Don't drown if you don't have to. I can still toss you a lifeline."

She didn't answer. Instead, she gestured to Hess who had wandered in and joined the crowd during the match. "Hess, reset the gravity field to standard."

"Aye, Sir."

As gravity deepened to a full 1g, Johnny felt the weight come back — in more ways than one. Dunning grabbed a towel, tossed him one too.

"Next time," she said, "don't run your mouth when sparring."

He caught the towel, grinning through the blood. "Next time, don't lie to me when you sweat."

She stopped at the edge of the mat. "Stick to plumbing and stop digging, Andretti."

"Funny thing," he said softly. "Most folks think plumbing is all about pipes, but digging's a big part of the job. Just ask any idiot with a backhoe who just severed a water main."

Dunning nodded and smiled slightly, "Backhoe. Yeah. That fits. You're an idiot with a backhoe. From now on, you're Backhoe."

As she walked off the mat, Hess glanced between them. He wasn't sure if he'd just seen a fight or foreplay.

Johnny pretended to shake out his hands. Inside, he wasn't thinking about his bruised ribs — he was replaying the look in her eyes when he said *worse.*

He'd seen that look before. On men who'd buried something they couldn't afford to have dug up. *Time to dig deep enough to break the water main, flood the hole, and see who comes up for air,* he thought.

22. Observation Post

Johnny closed Ham's notebook and set it to one side. "That's quite a story Ham," he said to the silence that surrounded him. He had decoded Ham's scribbling and transformed the notes into a new code, recording them digitally for later use, but only with his key.

In his mind, Johnny walked down a long hall. Closed red doors on each side, each with a brass plaque bearing names and numbers. He didn't need to open them. He'd filled each room and closed the door behind him when he'd finished a hit. At the end of the hall a grime-stained white door beckoned him. Johnny entered.

He placed Ham's notebook on a shelf and turned to study a mural – the whole picture of what Ham had revealed in his coded, bloodstained, un-hackable, paper notebook.

A galaxy spread across the wall. Around a distant sun labelled Thalyria circled Sanctum, Sanctifiers, and Consortium. Beyond Thalyria other suns gleamed, circled only by question marks. A line ran from Thalyria to the wreckage of a reconnaissance craft crashed into the Earth, where it whirled around Sol.

Within the circle of the Earth; UER, AguaLibre, and War of Unification with the words "China + USA" beneath them all. Lines ran from UER and AguaLibre to a cigar shape labeled Odyssey, where the name Ham appeared with lines from Ham to Farragut, Dunning, Rao, Grigson, Wu, Lafferty, Arnold, Hess, Kitchen Rat, Scarpo.

Another line arced from 'Odyssey' to a circle around Sol labeled 'The Belt.' Supplies, weapons, ice, and Living Water hung off that circle. Johnny studied the mural. It lacked a clear focal point. A smile missing from the face of the Mona Lisa.

The comm line Farragut insisted Johnny didn't have lit up, pulling Johnny out of his head. His eyebrows lifted sharply in surprise when he saw the caller ID.

"Hey Petie. Somebody die?" An unsolicited call from a mob boss was rarely a good thing.

"You tell me Johnny boy. I got an interesting call from a fellow you may know as Al? It seems that Al's nephew Jack Hamilton, has gone dark."

"Al?"

"Al. A-L." Petie had to spell it before Johnny caught the connection.

Al is AguaLibre. "Al is Jack's uncle?"

"Bingo." Petie's confirmation of the connection between Ham and AguaLibre set off the landing klaxons in Johnny's mental docking bay.

"Jack's … unable to write home."

"Busy, or dead?"

"Near enough to the latter. He's in medical quarantine. Doc says he may not make it."

"Is it contagious?"

"Maybe. Likely a couple more folks will fall out before Doc stops the illness. Give Uncle Al my contact info. I know what his nephew was sending. I'll make sure it keeps coming. I've got his nephew's family obligations in hand."

"Apologies Johnny. I got you this gig thinking it would be quiet for you. No idea you'd be so busy."

"No worries, Boss. I've got this. Funny thing, Petie. Water up here is like hootch during Capone's time."

Petie processed that reference for a moment. "Sounds fun. Need anything?"

"Glad you asked, Boss." He pressed a button on his communicator. "Just sent you a note. I'd really appreciate it if you could get that where it belongs and support my proposal. Here's some postage for you." Johnny pressed another button.

Petie looked at the readout below Johnny's image. The corner of his mouth lifted. "You think the freight on this is that heavy?"

"I hear UER Senators don't come cheap, even by the gross. This goes right, my contributions to your stamp collection could look like that every month."

"I'll do what I can." Petie paused. "Johnny, this play or yours, it's about as far from laying low as you can get. If Gambino finds you, the union won't be able to offer a relocation package." The words sent a small chill up Johnny's spine.

"Petie, this breaks my way, I'll square up with them over Vinnie's accident. If everyone stays mum about the green light you gave me, I'll sell them on self-defense, and pay the blood money out of my own pocket." *Or, I'll put them all in the ground,* he thought. *Having military black-ops contacts could be a serious dividend from this gig.*

The call ended. Johnny smiled. *Uncle Al?* For Johnny, the outreach of AguaLibre to the Mafia was the final connection he needed. Suddenly, the whole picture snapped into focus. He'd found the smile for his Mona Lisa.

Time to put that smile on my Mona Lisa – and see who finally recognized themselves in the picture.

23. Flipping

A holographic image of solar system from the sun beyond the Asteroid belt to include the Kuiper Belt hovered in the air before Admiral Phoss, Captain Farragut, and Johnny.

"You here to throw around more wild accusations, or have you solved the murder, Andretti?" Phoss was clearly in a mood.

"Good to see you too Admiral."

"Farragut?" Phoss growled.

"Andretti, you said you solved this murder."

"No Skipper, I said you and the Admiral would both want to hear my report. Because we have another big leak to stop. Only it ain't water that's spilling, it's truth. And if it gets out Earth is screwed."

"Cut the melodrama Andretti."

"I'll bottom line it for you Admiral."

"Please."

"The Consortium are conning you."

Two minutes of silence passed. When it was clear that Johnny wasn't going to add anything, unless they asked, Phoss broke the silence. "Why do you think that."

"Let me tell you a little story about my uncle, Fats. For health reasons, he moved to the uncivilized hinterlands of Montana and Idaho. Fats is a born hustler and an optimist.

Throw him into a pile of manure he finds a way to make it into money.

"A Montana hayseed griped about problems getting rid of piles of manure from his barn and corrals. Fats got himself a truck and charged Hayseed a small fee to haul off their piles. Fats trucks the crap to a fertilizer company and sells it to them. Soon he's hauling crap all over two states. Fats is getting paid coming and going. His game lasted until word got out and the fertilizer company started paying hayseeds directly for their manure."

"I care about Fats why?"

"UER is the hayseed struggling with dirty water. The Consortium is Fats. Odyssey is just one little Montana farmer. Every day the people of Earth generate about three hundred billion gallons of wastewater. That's a very big pile of manure. Wastewater treatment plants can't keep up with it. The AguaLibre folks began as eco-protestors over this ongoing flow of crap into the streams, rivers, and oceans."

"Trying to stay alive this far from all that water back on Earth, we are laser focused on recycling and reusing every drop. Uncle Fats sashays in and presto, Odyssey's water problems are solved. Next logical step is to scale up the operation."

Johnny paused to let his point sink in, then he moved on. "But my uncle got banished to Montana because he failed to see the big picture. The Consortium sees a bigger picture.

They're layering on a protection racket to help control their supply."

"The Consortium isn't extorting us for protection," Phoss fired back.

"No? Aren't they selling us tech to save us from Sanctifiers? The Consortium told us about the interstellar bogeymen, and tells us to play possum so we don't attract unwanted attention. They're providing us what we need, as long as we pay for their help." Johnny leveled his gaze at Phoss and Farragut. "Sound familiar gentlemen?"

They both nodded reluctantly.

"The reality is that there is plenty of water in the Belt. Thalyrians are taking water right here in the Belt. They're selling us our own water. Water scarcity is the first part of the Consortium scam, and AguaLibre has been co-opted into their control."

"The second part of their scam involves our dirty water; they call it 'Living Water,' and we're paying them to haul it off."

"Are you saying our sewage is their sacrament?" Phoss scoffed.

"I don't know if it's a mystical substance or a drug to them, but every ounce of our bio-matter mixed with water is extremely valuable. Like gold, gems, or illicit drugs."

"That's why Ham was holding vials of dirty water. Not to test. To use." Farragut confirmed.

"We're paying them to take away wastewater which they parcel into tiny vials and sell it to their Thalyrian market, and perhaps beyond, through their network of corner drug dealers. Profits from our wastewater are expanding Consortium power and influence in parts of the galaxy we haven't even imagined." Johnny went on. "What's more the Consortium and the Sanctifiers aren't dissidents and the legitimate government. They're two crime syndicates."

"That seems a stretch Andretti," Phoss dismissed.

"Admiral, of the three of us here, I'm the only one who has made a career inside a crime syndicate. I read their tells."

"Alright Andretti," Farragut conceded, "suppose you're right. What do we do about it?"

"We flip the con on them."

"How?"

"There are four pillars in the Consortium's con game.

"One: most people think the AguaLibre propaganda saying that alien interference in Earth politics is a tinfoil hat conspiracy theory. The Consortium wants to keep it that way, except for an 'elite' group of insiders who they want to manipulate. That story is true; making it easy for us to keep that going and use it to get inside AguaLibre and make them our unwitting double agent with the Consortium.

"Two: Most people believe the scarcity of water is a powerful factor limiting our ability to operate in space. They accept that purifying and recycling water is important. Again, we keep that sham going when the reality is we can't hardly bump into an asteroid without finding frozen water out here. Also, the fact that water-breathing Thalyrians are crossing immense distances between solar systems indicates that water supplies in space aren't much of a barrier.

"Three: Everyone believes that dirty water is wastewater, and a problem. Useless at best, poisonous at worst, unless it's cleaned and recycled. We keep that lie going too.

"Thalyrians, and maybe others, treasure our dirty water. Sanctifiers call *ensouled fluid.* To them, it's proof of life's divine spark. Earth's hydrosphere is the richest vein of Living Water in the galaxy, but the Consortium has kept that secret from their own zealots.

"So far, the scale of operation is tiny. Bay Sixteen is little more than a proof of concept; nowhere near the potential volume. We need to scale up the operation and make sure Earth benefits more than the Thalyrians.

"Four: Of those who know about the Thalyrians, most believe the Consortium is a valiant dissident organization trying desperately to help us avoid a terrible fate. That altruism allows our own zealots to justify nearly anything. Including killing millions to create the UER.

"A good reading of the intel gathered in the Bay Sixteen listening post shows …"

Farragut interrupted, "I never cleared you for that information."

Johnny continued as though Farragut hadn't spoken, "… Thalyrians are a society built on organized crime. Sanctifiers are the top 'family' right now; the Consortium has been a minor player. Steady access to Living Water is filling Consortium coffers; strengthening their hand.

"If the Sanctifiers find out about Earth, they will move in and destroy or take over the whole operation. When you're number one, you don't need to be subtle. Forcible subjugation will be their first plan. Down the road, if the Consortium gets powerful enough, they'll move on us just as hard as the Sanctifiers."

Farragut drew his own conclusion, "We break the Consortium hold over us by exposing the truth."

"No Skipper. It's critical to our survival that we appear naïve. When the illusion breaks, the story changes."

"Appear weak when you are strong, and strong when you are weak," Phoss quoted Sun Tzu. "The problem is we appear weak because we are weak. We need to get strong, and fast."

"Jujitsu doesn't depend on a lot of strength. It relies on leverage and using your opponent's momentum against them. A good con is a lot like that. It relies on leveraging a little bit of truth and using the power of your mark's beliefs against them."

"We keep pretending we believe all these lies; reinforcing the illusion or our ignorance while we build our strength."

"Exactly Skipper."

"Until then, the devil stays in the plumbing, and we're the only ones who know he's real," Phoss added.

"Right now, the thing we need most is time. Time to build a viable defense of our system." Farragut offered. "The Consortium has been helping us with that. But, if you're right,

Andretti, they won't risk losing their hold over us. They might help us become their muscle against the Sanctifiers, but only if they hold our leash."

"That dog won't hunt." Phoss snarled. "We're warriors. Not attack dogs."

"Better to die a lion than live as a dog." Farragut agreed and turned to Phoss, "Admiral, permission to read Andretti into the Suspenders program?"[13]

Phoss' face registered mild surprise, which turned to a little bit of cold humor, "Since he already tapped Bay Sixteen info, I suppose it's only a matter of time before he gets there himself. Permission granted."

Farragut pointed to the system holograph, "We've started with the Asteroid Belt," He tapped the image of the solar system, expanding the view outward from the Asteroid Belt to beyond the orbit of the outermost identified planets. "but if don't want alien invaders to use the outer planets as staging grounds against us, we need to go the Kuiper Belt as well."

"But before then, we need to complete flipping the con on the Consortium." Johnny jumped in. "We need a cover."

Phoss leaned back, "Why do I have the feeling you're about to con on us?"

---

[13] See Black Files: BF-U-001 Belts and No Suspenders. Technical Brief. Access Union

24. Inside Job

Johnny smiled. "Good instincts Admiral." All three heard the chime of the Admiral's comm line over the audio. At the same time, Johnny felt the vibration on his own line, letting him know a message had come in for him. Johnny sneaked a peek and smiled inwardly at the short message he read.

Phoss looked at his private display, then back to the conference video. "Excuse me gentlemen, I need to take this. Standby." The line went dead.

Farragut turned to Johnny. "I don't believe you've come in here with just an idea. I'd bet my stripes you've got something in motion already. Don't you?"

"Good instincts," Johnny repeated. The line lit up again.

"Space Plumbers Union?" Phoss glared at Johnny.

"I said we needed cover."

"What union?" Farragut queried.

"I don't know how he did it, but I suspect your plumber is behind this. It seems the AFL-CIO has founded a Space Plumbers Union with Andretti as its interim President. They've gotten recognition from the Senate and been unilaterally awarded the fluids management contracts for everything beyond the Earth's atmosphere. Even the 'miners' union and is on board." Phoss didn't sound pleased as he emphasized the miners union which was currently a front for the Corps of Engineers.

"Cheer up Admiral. You too Captain. You're both about to become very wealthy men. Unfortunately, it's going to look like you're on the take."

"I don't like the sound of that."

"Me either." Farragut agreed.

"Figured that," Johnny acknowledged. "The cover needs to look real. Hell, it needs to be real. Here's how it works." Johnny laid out his vision of the SPU and how it fit into the bigger picture. It was a little longer than an 'elevator speech,' but not much. When he was done Phoss and Farragut sat for a moment, absorbing it, staring at the edges, looking for cracks.

"So, your SPU installs and maintains fluid management packages in everything beyond Earth's atmosphere. The SPU operates a black market for water luxuries, ice, extra water rations, etcetera, everywhere it operates as well. Getting paid by the UER to install and operate their equipment. Getting paid by miners for black-market water. Meanwhile, the reality is that the water's being harvested by Thalyrians and sold to the SPU, which is marking it up? So, we are conning our own people?"

"If Earth stops believing water is scarce, the con collapses. Scarcity gives value, and credibility."

Phoss went on, "The SPU scales up the Bay Sixteen model. It gets paid by the UER to take wastewater, pretend to recycle it while swapping it for Thalyrian water deliveries, and instead sells it to the Consortium?"

"Some legitimate recycling happens. But, the Consortium needs to believe that we still think water is scarce and our wastewater is worthless. So, we scale the operation up to get more from them. We also flip some in the Consortium to get us access to other enemies of the Sanctifiers, who may be unwilling bedfellows of the Consortium. That gives us an avenue for tech the Consortium hasn't diluted. Tech that might be a game changer for our defenses and maybe even an offensive capability. Mostly funded by the Consortium payments for our wastewater."

"The SPU becomes our covert funding and operations organization. That is ambitious Andretti."

"The Space Plumbers Union builds the pipes. No one questions the plumber. We route the truth through the drains."

"The SPU's plumbing will run through every habitat, every processing hub. We'll own the pipes, the valves, and the data. That means we control what flows—and who drinks. With the credits, you can bankroll our black-budget agency without a single line item in the Assembly's oversight ledger." Farragut concluded.

"The Thalyrians have the Sanctifiers. We'll have the Sanitizers." Johnny grinned. "We clean up their mess, and use the profits to keep Earth from becoming their next parish."

"Andretti, why not run this play for yourself?" Farragut challenged.

"As President of the SPU, it looks like I'm doing just that, Skipper." Johnny paused a beat, then went on, "I've worked for predators all my life. I can smell the next one coming. The Consortium's not just trading—they're probing. They want control of the only thing they can't replicate: life. If we don't learn to fight in their currency, we'll drown in it."

"You really think this plumbing racket can bankroll a defense service?"

"It already has." Johnny tapped his wrist-com; the holo shifted to financial data. "Prototype contracts—Ceres, Vesta, Pallas. Each station's set to begin paying SPU for reclamation systems. Behind the scenes ten percent of the gross is diverted into a shadow fund tagged *maintenance reserves.* That's your seed money. Call it the Office of Strategic Sanitation."

Phoss chuckled, "Strategic Sanitation. God help me, I like it."

"Glad to hear that. I've already put both of your names on contracts and on the SPU oversight board. Accounts are already set up, and money has begun flowing into them. You do recall I mentioned that some folks will think you're on the take? This is their evidence. All legal, but smells a little like sewage."

Farragut snarled. "Explain to me why I have to get dirty for your con? I don't like that crap."

"Me either," Phoss agreed.

"I figured. See it from the Thalyrian viewpoint. The government is nothing more or less than the dominant mob family. To them, the UER is just a version of The Commission."

"The council of mob families that runs organized crime?"

"Exactly, Admiral. I see you've been reading up on the Mafia."

"A necessity when dealing with you."

"Also, when dealing with the Thalyrians," Johnny agreed. "Seeing you benefit from the con, reinforces their worldview. They understand graft, bribery, intimidation, and even murder as legitimate tools of their government, or their 'political party.' Knowing what you do about their hand in creating the UER already incriminates you. I'll make sure their channels understand that I am a career criminal. A made-man with worldwide connections to organized crime. For me to run a scalable black market for water in space with impunity is only believable if it also lines your pockets."

Johnny could see from the tight line of Farragut's mouth that he would prefer to gut Johnny on the spot than go along with this scheme.

"Captain, you've already shown you're willing to kill, and kill at scale, to protect what you value. Are you really balking at subterfuge to protect the people of Earth? With this you're still a warrior and becoming a spymaster."

The line of Farragut's mouth softened slightly, "You realize if this leaks, we're all dead—or worse, shamed and excommunicated by both everyone." Farragut growled.

"Then we keep it watertight, Skipper. We'll run the clean water up front, the dirty water out back, and keep the truth flowing to where we need it to be."

"What about the murder Andretti?" Phoss probed. "I realize this SPU is a big deal, but I don't like having this unsolved and I don't like trying to keep covering this up. Besides, if it persists much longer, Thalyrian's are going to start asking questions."

"I've all but solved the murder. If I'm right, the murderer did us all a favor. Regardless of motive or the unintended benefits to us, when I know the truth, the murderer and their victim will both become unfortunate victims of the same accident. Ham's body, and his killer's, will spin off into space. Even if, by some chance, their bodies are recovered, the evidence will support the accident. That'll make the cover up stick, but it won't go away."

"Easier to lie over time?"

"Time isn't the problem. The problem is too many people know Ham was murdered. There's the three of us along with Grigson, Wu, Lafferty, and the murderer."

"That's a lot of people to keep a secret." Phoss warned.

"Ben Franklin said the only way for three people to keep a secret is if two of them are dead." Farragut added.

"Space is a dangerous place, Skipper. There's room for more corpses in the space than all the swamps on Earth."

"I'm not going along with killing my staff, and threatening them might not go the way you think. Grigson and Wu are warriors. They've seen combat. All of them are fine officers. They won't talk."

"I have an idea about how we can handle Wu, Lafferty, and Grigson," Phoss offered. "Leave them to me."

"But we still have the murderer to deal with," Farragut objected.

"Leave the murderer to me. My suspects are down to one, and I'm about to get a confession."

"You know who it is?" Phoss exploded.

"I'll know when I hear the confession," Johnny reassured. *The trick is making sure somebody's still alive to give it.*

25. Confrontation

Johnny backed out of a crawlspace that passed through two decks before finding its way behind the bulkheads of Bay 16. He straightened and stretched, trying to pull the kinks out of cramped muscles.

He heard the sibilant 'snick' of the safety coming off a slug thrower. "Backhoe, you must have a death wish."

He turned. Dunning stepped from the shadows.

Johnny smiled. "Susan, you never disappoint me, do you? I'd hoped you would come alone."

His gaze dropped to the surprised "O" of the business end of a slug thrower with a sound suppressor on the end of the barrel. "We combining sparring with some range time now Susan?" Johnny gauged the distance between them. It was too far, he concluded. If she killed him and just left his body where it lay, it might be weeks before anyone found him in this seldom used passageway. She could be back on Earth, lost in the Belt, or just bluff it out on Odyssey.

"Why're you sticking your nose in this?"

"Skipper's orders."

"If you're military I'll eat your socks."

"I wasn't when I came aboard. You beating Ham to death threw quite a big wrench into my life. After that, my own smart mouth did the rest. Skipper drafted me with," Johnny paused, finally getting the joke, "with a taser."

"He used a taser on you? That doesn't sound like Farragut."

Johnny shook his head. "He used a regulation. Temporary Augmentation Zonal Reserve. TAZR allowed him to unilaterally induct me into the military as an officer. Then, he breveted me to Lieutenant Commander and made me his S2."

"Damn Johnny, you outrank me. If I get caught for this one, I'm doing hard time for sure."

Johnny shrugged. "In for a penny, in for a pound. Right? So, tell me, why kill Ham?"

"I should just kill you, now." The slug thrower held steady, aimed at Johnny's heart. She was a killer with excellent aim. A fast move would get him killed. Better to try talking.

"That would not be a good idea."

"For you?"

"For you. It wouldn't do me a lot of good either."

"Me?"

"Do you want to live your life looking over your shoulder. Never knowing when they are going to find and kill you?"

"The government wouldn't kill me. What I know is too valuable to them."

"I'm not talking about the government."

"Who then?"

"La Cosa Nostra."

"The Mafia? Why would they care?"

Johnny shrugged. "Because I'm what is called a 'made man.' I have put in place a Deadman switch that will let my associates know you did this. You kill me, they find out. Then, they kill you, your sister Sandra in Jakarta, her husband Dell, and their three kids. It's a matter of honor, and discipline."

"Mobsters get killed all the time."

"True, but if it isn't a cop, or a sanctioned hit, then whoever did it, is going to die. And, very possibly, everyone in their family as well. You a cop?"

She laughed. "You know I'm not."

Johnny shrugged. "There you have it."

"You're bluffing. You're no mafioso."

"Have it your way Susan, but before pull that trigger, ask yourself, do you really believe I'm a just a plumber?"

"You fix leaks like one."

Johnny smiled. "I love irony. What can I say? I'm the kind of plumber the mob brings in when they need a human leak fixed. Imagine my surprise when Farragut drafted me to fix this leak?"

"Farragut knows you're a hitman?"

"Not at first. However, just like you, the situation required me to *read him in.* I needed to make it clear that spacing me because I know too much wasn't one of his cleanup options."

Dunning replayed in her head all the moves Johnny had made and the secrets he had uncovered. His hand-to-hand combat skills and weapons handling were at least as good as her own. She figured all Johnny's talk about military rank might just be more evidence of how widely read he was, but if it were true, it did put a different complexion on things.

"I killed Ham because he knew too much, and he was going to tell the wrong people."

"He was a leak."

Dunning nodded.

"Who are the wrong people?"

"You know he was a gill-head, right?"

"You saying you killed him because he was palling around with AguaLibre?"

"The dissidents? No. I actually kind of like them. I have some friends who've gone underwater. This whole 'United Earth Republic' is papering over an authoritarian oligarchy."

"Then why bring it up?"

"Because Ham was *born* with gills. He was an alien. A Thalyrian. And, he was spying for them."

"Sanctifier or Consortium?"

Dunning's mouth fell open for a moment. She recovered. "You know about them?"

Johnny nodded. "Which bunch was he working for?"

"Does it matter?"

"Not to me."

"I think he worked for both. But officially he was a Sanctifier. And you're right. It didn't matter. He knew something that we don't want any Thalyrians to know."

"Belts and Suspenders?"

Again, Dunning was stunned for a moment. "You know about that?"

"It was one of my early discoveries. I thought Farragut and his pals were looking to pull a coup." Johnny's embarrassment at getting that wrong came through in his shrug. "You can't get 'em all right."

"I figured that was important enough to kill him."

"I agree. However, when you stop a leak, doing the whole job requires you clean up the whole mess."

"What do you mean?"

"Who was his handler and how did Ham plan to get his info off the station? The easiest way to get those answers was from Ham. Fixing the leak means stopping the flow of information. With Ham dead, that's harder."

"I see that," she conceded.

"I get *why* you killed Ham. But, why did *you* kill him? Why not run it up the chain? You worried about other leaks?"

"This platoon, this post, this secret, it's my first command. It's my job to protect and defend, *all* of it."

"Duty?" Johnny shook his head. "What you did with that wrench wasn't duty. That was rage."

"I had to hide the gills…"

Johnny shook his head. "That wasn't all of it."

Dunning's finger caressed the trigger. Johnny got ready to move. At this distance, he knew he didn't have much chance, but he wasn't going to surrender to his fate.

"You ask too many questions, Backhoe."

Silence stretched between them.

He saw the corner of her mouth turn down. *This is it,* he thought.

"A lot of anger," she admitted. "Unification caught me off guard. One day it was 'support, protect, and defend the Constitution of the United States of America.' I was raised on 'we pledge our lives, our fortunes, and our sacred honor.' In the blink of an eye our government sets aside all that and joins with China to roll out the UER. That hurt. It made me angry too."

"But you earned a chest full of medals fighting for the UER?"

"I did. I bled for it. I killed for it. I know it is a bit of a sham. But, when I understood the Thalyrians, … there is no way in Hell I'm going to let that bunch of thugs and criminals make us their bitches. Not on my watch."

"And now, you tell me you're a mobster like them. What am I supposed to do with that Backhoe? How are you any different than those gill heads?

Johnny smiled sadly. "I'm not sure if I'm different, Susan. Maybe I'm not. But, I can tell you this. As long as I'm alive, I'm going to do what I can to keep humanity from being owned by the Thalyrians, or anyone like them."

Dunning's thumb flicked the safety on the slug thrower. She set it on the deck and kicked it across to him. "Now you're taking me in and putting me on trial, eh Backhoe?"

"That could be awkward."

"Could you be more vague?" Dunning chuckled dryly.

"Publicly acknowledging Thalyrian involvement would be an epic crap-storm." He picked up the gun and turned it on her, slipping the safety off.

"If I'd known you were going to space me, I wouldn't have surrendered."

"Spacing you would be the easy call," Johnny admitted, holding the slug thrower steady on Dunning.

They stared at each other a moment. Resignation began to make Dunning's shoulders sag just a little. "Ham, or whatever his real name was, was a Sanctifier. Like you, he figured out what's going on with the Belt. He also uncovered our deal with the Consortium. I don't think he managed to tell anyone. I figured he was going to tell the Sanctum and bring on their invasion. If I delayed that even a little, it was worth it."

"Why don't you think he got word out?"

Dunning reached into a pocket and pulled out an inch square gray box. She bent and slid it across the deck to his feet. Johnny picked it up and pocketed it.

"Ham had that in hand when I killed him. It fits the profile of a Thalyrian communicator. We've been monitoring their comms and would probably have detected his transmission. But that would have been too late."

"What if Ham was Consortium, or a double agent?"

"Sanctifiers, Consortium. They're two sides of the same coin. The entire Thalyrian civilization is a collection of mobsters. It's their history. The Sanctifiers just happen to be more powerful than the Consortium, so they're on top right now. The rest of the galaxy hates them both, but the other systems can't stop fighting each other long enough to join forces and stamp them out."

"You know this how?"

"Two sources. One was Ham. I befriended him, before I killed him."

"And he told you the Sanctifiers are criminals?"

"Not in so many words. I listened to him. For a spy, he was very chatty. And the mind his words revealed was crooked, criminal, exploitative, brutal, and ruthless."

Johnny filed that one away to revisit later. "You mentioned two sources?"

"The downed scout ship allowed us to clone their receivers and transmitters. I don't think they counted on that. We learned to translate Thalyrian fast. It isn't too hard. Their codes were only marginally harder. We aimed some listening devices their way. Thalyrians are a bunch of Chatty Kathys. Not only did we snag their military signals, we got commercial ones as well. Quantum communications bring us their signals in real time.

"Mainstream media may give a skewed view, but it can still be informative. Thalyrian movies, news broadcasts, even their sitcoms have been a revelation and a massive source of context. We learned about their society and a good bit of their history."

That explains the massive amounts of intel I found on the Thalyrians, Johnny thought to himself. Out loud he said,

"Good work. Working closely with Ham, I suspected as much myself."

"Of course you did. It takes one to know one."

"I'll take that as a compliment."

"Don't."

Johnny shrugged and smiled. "Dunning, what do you think about dying in an accident?"

"That wouldn't be my first choice. Is there another alternative?"

"Plenty. Some are a lot worse."

"Like what?"

"Life in a black site prison comes to mind."

"Where there's life, there's hope."

"Voluntary death liberates your soul."

"I don't think Buddha ever said anything like that."

"Nietzsche. Or the U.S. Marshalls Service. I forget which."

Dunning laughed, "Are you going to hit me with some crazy twist and tell me you're actually an undercover lawman?"

"That would be quite a twist. But, no. Not a lawman. Hear me out, Susan. I think you'll agree it's best if you croak. Accidentally, of course."

"Of course."

Somewhere behind the bulkheads, a pump kicked in. The ship held its breath. So did Susan.

26. Hit the Fan

Two days later the proverbial crap hit the fan. The sharp and reverberating klaxon tone signaling a hull breach reverberated throughout the Odyssey. The words, "This is not a drill," sent chills down everyone's spine.

Military and civilians alike rushed to their emergency stations, waiting tensely for further instructions. Fight or flight urges pushed their hearts to the limit. After what seemed hours, but was more like about fifteen minutes, the 'all-clear' sounded.

Chattering nervously, like leaves on a breeze tickled tree, people from end to end of Odyssey tried to return to what they had been doing before the unexplained alarm. Hours later, Captain Farragut's voice surged through ship-wide comms, preceded by the ships-whistle calling everyone to attention.

"I regret to announce that earlier today we lost two crew members to a hull breach. Marine Lieutenant Susan Dunning and the civilian plumber Jack Hamilton were both killed instantly in what appears to have been an accident. Civilian plumber John Andretti survived the incident with minor injuries. Odyssey is secure. That is all."

The real alarms went off inside the mind of one man, hours before the blaring of the ship's klaxon.

Scarpo had just returned from the communal shower. Towel wrapped around his narrow hips. His lean form chiseled from constant training. Shower shoes on his feet making a slight slapping noise as he walked. Civilians called them flip flops. Marines called the rubber slabs with toe straps shower shoes. Scarpo's shower and shave kit dangled easily from one hand.

The door clicked shut with an odd finality as Scarpo stepped into the narrow berth he shared with three other Marines. His roommates were on duty, so Scarpo had the room to himself. Or so he believed.

As soon as the door locked Scarpo knew he wasn't alone. He started to turn and look into the only shadowed area of the room.

"Don't," was all Johnny said.

Scarpo stopped in mid-motion, hearing the distinctive 'snick' of metal on metal as the safety slid off a slug thrower.

"You got some balls Plumber," Scarpo growled. "I'm gonna feed em to ya after I cut 'em off."

"In a little while Rao may call you and ask you to come with him to take care of me. Ignore the call, or tell him no."

"Why would I do that?"

"He's meeting me on my ground. If I see you anywhere nearby, you're dead. Now, put your shower kit on top of your head and hold it there with both hands while counting backwards from one hundred."

"Like Hell." Scarpo felt a slight needle jab in his neck. He hadn't even heard the Plumber move. Scarpo spun to try to grapple with the older man. The room was empty except for himself. That was the last thing he saw before he collapsed on the floor. He was awakened nearly an hour later by the buzz of his communicator. It was Rao.

"Where the hell you been Scarpo? It's time to deal with the Plumber."

Scarpo looked around the room, it was still locked from inside and there was no sign the Plumber had ever been there. A chill ran down his spine and suddenly he could smell the sour scent of fear rolling off his own body. An elixir for him when he smelled it on others, his own fear made his stomach roil. "Today doesn't work for me. If this is your chance, then do it yourself."

The surveillance device planted in Scarpo's room transmitted the conversation to Johnny. By then, he was already stalking Rao.

Rao smirked as he passed the rack of pressure suits staged at the interior base of the cylinder that both housed the equipment for, and the access to exterior gun blister 61.

"Those would just prolong my agony if there's a hull breach," he mused. For a moment he had a vision of himself in a pressure suit, floating in space; hoping in vain for rescue while his meager supply of air ran out and he suffocated. "Nope. Better to go fast." He stepped through the access opening and pulled the hatch shut behind him. "No sense letting the old man know I'm here ahead of him and better to muffle any sound of what's to come." He patted the lump of the slug thrower in his pocket. Then, he began climbing up the narrow ladder.

He was more than halfway up the spiraling ladder when he heard the loud click of the hatch closing behind him at the entrance to the cylinder. Rao smiled, congratulating himself for his foresight in arriving ahead of the Plumber.

Johnny lifted his finger from the button that triggered the magnetic closure of the hatch and waited for Rao to enter the blister.

As his head and shoulders emerged from the ladder-well into the gun blister Rao felt someone grab his collar from behind and strike him hard on the back of the head. He vaguely felt the edges of the hatch scraping his ribs and legs as he was lifted roughly through the opening and tossed to the floor where he slumped, senseless.

Johnny quickly secured Rao's hands and feet, then covered his mouth. After positioning Rao exactly where he desired, he taped a bag of blood onto his chest and then revived the young man by waving smelling salts under his nose. "Wakey, wakey my little water rat." Johnny taunted.

The outer bulkhead of the gun blister pressed cold against his back. With a cough and shake of his head, Rao regained consciousness. The first thing he saw made him recoil in horror. The air here was chill and his panicked breathing quickly created a small cloud of vapor.

Ham's body, unpacked from a storage can and sliced for autopsy was suspended from a thin cord a few feet in front of his face. Johnny had convinced Wu to forego stapling or suturing shut the autopsy cuts. After bringing Ham's body to the turret, he had dressed the dead man and then made cuts in his clothes to roughly align with those of the cadaver.

To Rao, it looked like Ham had been sliced open and gutted. His barely recognizable face was a pulp of bone and flesh with his eyes at odd angles, staring at Rao. Rao's eyes rolled back in his head as he started to pass out. Johnny's hard slap to his face brought him back to full consciousness. Eyes impossibly wide in fear, Rao looked from Ham to Johnny, and back.

"Don't worry. Ham didn't feel much of that. I can't say the same for you though."

Rao whined around his gag.

"You're a leak, Rao. I'm a plumber. Fixing leaks is what I do."

"Waw?" Even through the gag Rao's question was clear.

"Why? Because you're greedy, stupid, and careless. Whatever you did back in the slums of Rio, if you'd stayed, they would have ended up killing you. You're a massive liability to any criminal or clandestine enterprise. If I don't do this now, it's only a matter of time before you say the wrong thing to the wrong person and get us all killed or tossed into prison."

"M. Mm." He shook his head in denial.

"Did you know Ham was an alien? A Thalyrian Sanctifier."

Rao's eyes went wide in surprise. He shook his head no.

"You know about the Thalyrians, right?"

He shrugged.

"You should've believed the AguaLibre stories. Ham was spying for them. Water theft was part of his cover. He used it to get close to you. And he used you to get information. You knew about the weapons going out to the Belt?"

Rao nodded.

"Did you ever tell Ham about the weapons and where they were headed?"

Rao shook his head.

"This is important Rao. Don't lie to me about this. Did you ever mention anything to Ham about the weapons, or the extracurricular activities along the Belt?"

Rao shook his head violently.

"Did he ever say anything to you, or ask you anything about the weapons, the Belt, or Bay Sixteen?"

"Mma. Ixtnn."

"He asked you about Bay Sixteen?"

Rao nodded.

"What did you tell him?"

"Mmmng." Rao shook his head.

"You didn't give up the ice-game, the communications, or the research going on in Bay Sixteen?"

"Mmm Mm." He shook his head. "Mm nn nmnm." His eyes rolled in disdain.

"Yes, Rao. You are stupid. That's why you thought you could cheat me on the water theft, intimidate me with Scarpo, and kill me with this." Johnny held up the small slug thrower he had removed from Rao after knocking him out.

"Did you think for a minute what would happen up here if you missed me, or if the round went all they way through me?" Johnny pocketed the gun and waved a hand at the bulkhead behind Rao. "Do you know what's behind you? A few centimeters of armor and then the vacuum of space for millions of miles."

"You didn't even consider that you might rupture the bulkhead with a slug did you? You didn't even bother with a pressure suit." Johnny shook his head in disgust. "You're not stupid Rao. You'd need at least 50 more IQ points to get up to the level of stupid. You're the village idiot."

Rao scowled.

"When that bulkhead behind you ruptures, this room will violently decompress. All the air and any loose objects in the room will try to get out of that hole at the same time. Most of that will be violently ejected into space, pulled through a hole so small that all those objects will get ripped apart and smashed together, at the same time. Perhaps there will be enough surface area, mass, and remaining air to plug the hole and create a temporary seal. Regardless, I carry a seal kit anytime I work along the outer hull. I also always don a pressure suit when working along the outer hull. And," Johnny pointed to a steel cable from his safety belt to a stanchion on edge of the hatch, "I use a safety line,"

Johnny walked over and closed the hatch to the chamber. "That's another safety precaution I always follow."

He turned and pointed to a high-pressure line. "That green hose is unique. It has about forty-five thousand pounds of pressure per square inch. It fires a mild, abrasive into the barrel of this cannon to clear it of small debris after each shot."

"You see that red spot?" He pointed to a dull red patch on the otherwise green line. "That's what happens when important things get built by the lowest bidder. Ham patched that leak three months ago. When it leaked, under half pressure it scored that hull plate directly behind you, but not enough to justify replacement. Unfortunately for you, this hose is now under full pressure and about to break again. I know it's breaking because," he pulled a small fluid dispenser out of a pocket of his suit. "I'm going to apply this solvent which will interact with the patching compound and to make it, and the hose brittle enough that when I grab it, the hose will break and the highly pressurized fluid will shoot out at the bulkhead there."

He pointed to a spot near Rao's head. "It will look like the hose struck out like a very angry snake and ripped a hole in the hull. I'm certain that will happen because the ablative I strapped to Ham's back is going to react with the fluid as it slices through him to ensure the mass, friction, and pressure are sufficient to slice the already weakened armor behind you. After a few seconds the auto-clamp will cut the flow and the pressure in the line will abate. But by then, it will be too late for poor Ham, and you. I'll manage to get the hole sealed and barely escape with my life, but … you understand what becomes of you and Ham. Right?"

Johnny donned the helmet of his pressure suit, checked the O2 tank and his anchor cable one more time. Then he applied the liquid from the small bottle onto the reddish area of the patch. It immediately began to change color. He heard Rao trying to scream behind his gag, but didn't look away from his task.

In less than three minutes everything had happened just as Johnny had said it would. Klaxons were still sounding, but they would stop as soon as the sensors detected that the ship was no longer venting atmosphere into space.

Johnny gathered up the final trace evidence of Rao's murder and reopened the pressure hatch. Climbing through it, he closed it behind him and descended the ladder to the access hatch. Again, he opened and passed through it, closing it behind him. The two closed hatches would absolutely protect the station from further air loss if his temporary hull seal failed.

Only when the second hatch closed firmly did Johnny take off his pressure helmet and open a comm line to the bridge. "Bridge, this is John Andretti. Ham and I, with Marine Lieutenant Dunning on security were attempting to repair a pressure line in gun turret 61 when it ruptured and breached the hull. Between the high-pressure fluid jet and the explosive decompression, Dunning and Ham were killed instantly. I managed to stop the leak and put a temporary seal on the hull breach. I need medical and engineering at my location immediately."

"This is the bridge," came the crisp reply. "Acknowledged. Medical and Engineering are being dispatched to your location."

"Andretti." Captain Farragut's steely tones rang out over the line. "Did you just blow a hole in one of my gun turrets, and kill two of my crew?"

"That's one way to see it Skipper."

"There's another way?"

"I just plugged a leak that could've gotten more folks killed."

"I thought Mister Hamilton was quarantined in Sick Bay."

"He got better. Must have checked himself out? All I know is that he showed up ready for work, just in time for a job that needed both of us."

Sneaking the container with Ham's body out of Sick Bay was easier than getting it in, unnoticed. He showed up in Med Bay with a work order for bio-hazard disposal. Wu had already re-packaged the dead plumber. Wu then forged a self-checkout log entry for the dead plumber to offset the admitting order and Griggson adjusted the time stamp to fit the required timeline.

Seeing Johnny carting away a container of biohazard material wasn't noteworthy for the medical staff, most of whom considered Johnny a glorified janitor.

"Report to my Ready Room as soon as Medical releases you. Understood?"

"Yep Skipper. You're number one on my list after the Doc clears me." Johnny smiled to himself as he fancied he could hear Farragut growl in irritation at his distinctly unmilitary response. He couldn't bring himself to give Wild Bill the satisfaction of an 'aye, aye, sir.'

Beneath his calm demeanor, Johnny was squirming like a cat in a dog kennel. *I'm not a casualty yet,* Johnny told himself, *but I've never before had to sell my stories in front of a judge. Judges killed more people than hitmen.*

Act V The Con is On

Figure 5 Hull Breach

27. Inquest

"What the Hell happened in there Andretti?"

They were in the Captain's Ready Room. Johnny was in the 'hot seat' directly in front of Farragut's desk. Grigson, Wu, and Lafferty were seated in a row to one side. Farragut was behind his desk with Admiral Phoss looking over his shoulder via video link. Although it was Farragut's show, Phoss's presence made Johnny feel uncomfortably like he was in a courtroom with the judge looking down at him.

"Skipper, I hope you have the recorders on because I really don't want to have tell this story more than once."

Farragut pointed to the dim red light on the panel near his hand. "It was on before you entered. Now, let's have it straight. No window dressing. This is an official inquest, and this taping will be reviewed by JAG. This is all 'on the record' Mister Andretti."

"Got it," Johnny nodded his understanding. This was going on the public record, as authoritative as a trial transcript. He had one take to get this right. He resisted the urge to glance at Wu, Grigson, and Lafferty. They needed to stick to their scripts, or the whole thing would blow up. After decades with "No witnesses," as his guiding principle, Johnny was deeply uncomfortable that now, he had to rely on witnesses to prevent his exposure. He let that discomfort show just enough to reinforce the image that he was traumatized by what had happened.

In an unusual gesture of compassion, Farragut poured a glass of water and pushed it across his desk toward the plumber. "Take your time Mister Andretti. I realize this has been a very rough day for you. Everyone else here has already been in situations like you were in today. We know how hard it can be."

Harder than you know, Johnny thought. He picked up the glass and took a hasty gulp, reinforcing the image of a rattled civilian which he and Farragut had orchestrated.

"Ham and I were doing some work on an extremely high-pressure system that cleans the gun bore in Blister Sixty-

One. The work required both of us. Because those compartments are classified, Dunning escorted us."

"For the record Mister Andretti, who are you referring to?"

"Sorry Skipper, er Captain. Jack Hamilton, Ham, is … was … my Journeyman Plumber and Marine Lieutenant Susan Dunning."

"Proceed."

"Dunning went into the ladderwell and gun blister first. Ham and I followed and waited, on the ladder just outside the blister itself, until she gave us the all-clear. Ham climbed through the hatch ahead of me. I had just entered the blister and snapped my safety line to the hatch anchor when the hose we were there to fix ruptured."

Johnny shakily gulped some more water and set the glass down on Farragut's desk. "The first jet from the line was so powerful it cut through Ham and Dunning and blasted a six-foot gash in the outer hull. I was sure I was next. It takes longer to tell you about it than it took to happen. The safety pressure valve kicked in and stopped the flow through the hose, but it was too late for Ham and Dunning."

Johnny took another drink.

"Everybody here knows about explosive decompression from a hull breach. Everything not tied down was sucked out through the breach and into space."

Johnny paused again and stared across the room at the porthole in the bulkhead, a 'thousand-yard stare.'

"When I was twelve my old man did maintenance at the North Pier pump station. Big brine-return line from the cannery ran under the pier into a header box, then out through a slot that was maybe six feet long and two inches wide. Looked harmless—like a mail slot. 'Harmless'll kill you,' Dad told me.

"They were swapping an impeller and had the tide-side gates cracked just enough to keep the box from going dry. You could feel the pull in your teeth. Dad didn't lecture—he showed. He tossed in a length of dock line to 'see if the grate's clear.' Rope hit the water, turned, and then it just… vanished. Not down like a drain—flat, sideways, like a zipper closing. Twelve feet of rope gone in one breath. The frayed end came back out of the slot like spaghetti—same rope, new shape.

"The foreman added a broom handle—old hickory, not cheap. It drifted toward the slot, hesitated, and then the tip found the pressure edge. The handle didn't break where you'd think; it splintered in slivers along the grain and the pieces shaved themselves thin enough to slide through the two-inch letterbox. Sounded like a handful of pencils snapping inside a muffler.

"They kept a crate of 'teaching junk' for new guys—webbing, a rubber boot, a sack of bolts. Webbing went through like ribbon. The boot folded flat, sole first, then the upper followed like a tongue in a press. The bolts didn't go through; they ricocheted in the box and turned the inside into a bell. Everyone took a step back without being told.

"Dad pointed at the slot. 'Water's incompressible,' he said. 'Force scales with speed squared. Give it a long edge and a narrow gap and it becomes a cutter and a vacuum at the same time.' Then he looked at me to make sure I was hearing the part under the words. 'If you give it a body, it'll find the soft joints first. Elbows, knees, anything that can fold. Tools go in with you and come out as shrapnel. That's why we tag-out, tie-off, and keep our distance.'

"That gap in the hull was only two inches. I hear that, I see that, and I see Ham and Dunning, just like that rope turn into noodles and the broomstick into confetti. Doesn't matter if you're a man or a mule—six feet by two inches at that flow is a garbage disposal with a sense of direction. You don't win a fight with it. You decide not to start one."

Johnny let his gaze come back to the present, sliding across the faces of his audience. All were slightly ashen.

"Fortunately for me my tether held. Otherwise, I would probably have been killed as well. I managed to close the faceplate on my pressure suit. With no more air pressure in the blister, I was able to throw a temporary hull patch over the breach. The hose was drained up to the stop valve by then too. It wasn't a long length of hose to empty, but those pumps are powerful, and the hose was long enough." Johnny shook his head and sipped some water.

"I re-pressurized the blister and went back down the ladder to the passageway. That's when I notified the Bridge." He shot a look at Lafferty. "I guess I should have told Engineering first. Commander Lafferty said something about using my body to seal the next hull breach if I didn't follow proper protocol next time there was a problem."

Farragut smiled slightly. "In fairness to Mister Lafferty I was less than patient with her when the alarms went off and she didn't have any answers for me."

Farragut turned to Lafferty. "Commander Lafferty, what did your engineering analysis of the scene reveal?" Johnny was unconcerned about what Lafferty had to say. Physics and facts were all on his side.

"Sir, the break in the bore line was on top of the prior leak. The hull breach was consistent with an outward blast and a cut from highly pressurized fluids. Mister Andretti's repair was made with standard breach expedient materials from his kit. The safety latches secured the space until pressure was stabilized. I could go on, but the short version is that everything supports the plumber's story." Her reply was crisp, but Johnny noted her clenched jaw and fists throughout. She seemed on the edge of exploding.

"Commander Wu, what did your forensic analysis of the scene discover?" Johnny didn't worry about Wu's testimony of the scene either. The forensics were simple chemistry. The dicey part was getting a dead man to 'walk out' of the Med Bay and into the gun blister.

"Unfortunately, Captain, the chemicals in the expedient breach seal are extremely caustic. Even when Commander Lafferty brought me the damaged hull panel after it was replaced, I cannot positively tell you the identity of anyone pulled through that breach. Inside the blister I found trace DNA from Mister Andretti, Mister Hamilton, Lieutenant Dunning, Specialist Three Raoni, and at least six other crew members who have logged time there, but weren't present during the incident."

"Your conclusion?"

"I found nothing to contradict Mister Andretti's testimony, sir."

"Commander Grigson. You conducted an electronic audit of the scene. What did you find?"

Johnny knew that here was where the heavy-duty deceit was about to debut. Judicious doctoring of old and new footage had forced Grigson and Johnny to work closely for several hours.

Grigson used his wrist unit and pulled up video recordings with audio. "Sir, I began my timeline with Mister Hamilton checking himself out of the Med Bay. You can see here that he slipped out of the Med Bay while the crew on duty happened to be looking away." The video showed Ham walking casually out of the Med Bay. In the background, the staff had their backs toward him and were focused on the birthday cake offered to a member of their team. "This was at zero one seventeen. Just five minutes before that I found a record of a communications call from Mister Hamilton to Mister Andretti."

"Oh, that's right. I forgot to mention that." Johnny ducked his head in embarrassment. "Ham called me and said he was sick of being sick and ready to get back to work. He'd seen the open ticket for Blister 61 and he offered to join me.

He felt guilty that he hadn't already made time to replace that hose."

Farragut nodded. "Commander, please continue."

"Aye sir. Badge and visual records show Mister Hamilton entering the Plumbers Closet and leaving shortly after with his toolkit, in the company of Mister Andretti." *A very frequent scene in the weeks before Ham's death,* Johnny added mentally.

The screen filled with a shot of Ham and Andretti, suited up for work and walking together away from the Plumber's Closet with the appropriate time stamp glowing faintly in the corner.

Grigson fast forwarded. "Logs show that Mister Andretti contacted Lieutenant Dunning and she then met the two plumbers just outside the access hatch for Blister 61." *The call to Dunning was legit,* Johnny added to his mental narrative.

The scene shifted to the passageway with the Blister 61 access hatch clearly marked and the timestamp showed clearly.

Grigson narrated, "We see the Lieutenant enter the ladderwell hatch followed shortly by the plumbers. Mister Andretti appears to be the only person donning a pressure suit. Inside the ladderwell and the blister itself are classified spaces, so no video there."

"Fast forward and a few moments later, we see the hull breach alarms go off and the access hatch in the passageway slams shut and seals on its own."

"Fast forwarding again, about ten minutes later, the alarms stop and shortly after that Mister Andretti opens the access hatch from inside the ladderwell. He clears the hatch and seals it behind him with a security code. Then we have his call to the Bridge to report the breach."

"Your conclusion Commander?"

"All the operational information we have supports Mister Andretti's account." This was the most dangerous part of the lie. A zealous investigator could detect their edits and might find recordings of Rao approaching the blister. Grigson had noted the odd gaps Johnny had engineered by looping selected camera feeds and erasing others. He knew the lie was deeper than it appeared. He followed Farragut's orders and helped Johnny falsify the evidence.

"Admiral Phoss, I am prepared to rule that Mister Hamilton and Lieutenant Dunning have died in the line of duty due to an accidental hull breach caused by the rupture of a failed hydraulic line in Blister Six One. Do you concur?"

"I concur Captain."

Farragut nodded slowly. "Mister Andretti, it sounds like your quick action saved us from more damage. There's probably a commendation in it for you."

"Just doing my job Skipper."

Farragut nodded and turned off the recording. "Aw shucks Johnny, you're too modest," he snarled sarcastically. "Now, let's hear the truth. Everyone here knows that Ham was dead long before this hull breach. What really happened?"

"Everyone here read in on Belts and Suspenders, and Bay Sixteen?" Johnny challenged.

"Go ahead Captain," Phoss nodded.

Moments later, the conversation again focused on Johnny.

"The short version is that I lured Dunning there and confronted her. She confessed to killing Ham."

"Dunning? No way," Lafferty nearly exploded, all the pent up tension showing in her body poured out in a firehouse blast of words. "Captain Farragut, you know how closely Susan and I have been working together for nearly three years now. You know what we've done and the hours we worked side by side. She can kill. But she would never murder anyone."

"Don't take my word for it. I recorded her confession." Johnny pushed a button on his wrist unit and Dunning's face appeared.

"I killed Ham because he knew too much, and he was going to tell the wrong people."

Lafferty's mouth fell open.

Johnny stopped the recording. "I can play the rest for you, but the short version is that she figured out Ham was a Thalyrian spy, working for the Sanctifiers. He figured out that Belt operations were about a lot more than mining and that UER was working with the Consortium."

Johnny touched another button and the recording of Dunning fast forwarded and stopped as she said, "I figured that was important enough to kill him." The video conveniently showed no background details to contradict Johnny's assertions of time and location.

"Dunning's combat experience taught her that a single kill-shot could save many lives. I don't believe she thought of this as murder. Killing Ham was her on overwatch, dropping a bad guy before the bad guy did any damage. But, the attack wasn't pre-planned. She hadn't thought through. Moments after she stopped him from exposing this operation, I pinged Ham's locator. I accidentally stampeded her. She thought I was nearby. She panicked and slipped out through an air duct."

"I had figured out most of this before she and I met in Blister 61. It was a real repair, but I used it as a pretext to confront her. I brought Ham's body for shock value to prompt her confession."

"You killed her," Grigson snarled. "No trial. You acted as judge, jury, and executioner. And, I just helped you cover it up."

Lafferty's body tensed again.

Johnny shook his head, his face a picture of sorrow. "I think she was willing to face this, even though she brought a gun to kill me," Johnny pulled Susan's slug-thrower out of his pocket and slid it across Farragut's desk. "You'll find her prints and mine on that."

"You took that from her?" Grigson was incredulous.

"No, she surrendered it," Johnny replayed the part of his tape where she handed over the sidearm. "But, before we could talk more, the hose ruptured and she was killed."

"More likely, you killed her," Lafferty voiced the skepticism evident on the faces of all three officers.

"And all of you," Farragut turned to Wu, Lafferty, and Grigson. "on my orders, collaborated with Mister Andretti to manipulate the evidence to support his story. That puts all of us in the same life raft with Andretti. Understood?"

Slowly, they all nodded.

"And the body of Mister Hamilton. Where is it?"

"Just like I said, Skipper. When that hose broke," Johnny paused, "Hell, I'm lucky I didn't end up as chop suey down the disposal along with Ham and Dunning."

"Captain," Admiral Phoss interrupted. "I need to commandeer the rest of this interview."

"Acknowledged."

Phoss turned his gaze on Andretti and the Commanders. "The report you have just heard about the real events that occurred in Blister 61 and the fate of Dunning and Hamilton are all classified Ultra Top Secret. Do you understand?"

They nodded.

"I need to hear you say it." Individually they each asserted their understanding.

"Thank you. Now, listen carefully. Each of you has a choice to make today which will affect the rest of your lives. Your first option is to live with being surveilled forever. Anything you say or do that looks like it would reveal the truth about the nature and fate of Mister Hamilton will cause you to disappear into a black site prison, court-martialed and executed for treason." Phoss paused to let his first option sink in.

"Your second option is to enter a newly formed clandestine service of the UER. Outwardly, you will continue your careers while you secretly carry out the work necessary to keep the people of Earth safe from threats from the denizens of other systems. Discovery in your new role will likely result in torture and death. Do you understand these options?"

Grigson, Wu, and Lafferty vocally confirmed. Johnny remained silent. Grigson raised an eyebrow and glared at him.

Phoss went on. "Those of you choosing the first option, say aye." Silence. "Those of you choosing the second option, say aye." The three dutifully responded with an aye.

Grigson pointed at Johnny. "What about the plumber?"

"Excellent question Mister Grigson. The plumber, as you call him, is your new boss."

"The hell you say," Grigson growled.

"He reports to Captain Farragut and to me. If you don't find that acceptable, Mister Grigson, we can move on to the black site prison directly, if you prefer?"

"We're Commanders in the UER Space Navy. We can't work for a civilian."

"Need I remind you Mister Grigson, that the Consuls are civilians and we all work for them?"

"That's different."

"I thought some of you might feel that way." Phoss pressed a button and all of their communicators chimed. "For that, and other reasons, the Consuls prepared this."

Everyone paused a moment to read, and absorb the shock. Wu spoke first, "The Commandant of Marines is going ballistic when he sees this."

"Damn straight," Lafferty agreed, shaking her head.

Grigson read the message and stared in disbelief. "A Marine Colonel? An O6, just like that? Captain, are you okay with the plumber having the same rank as you?"

Johnny read the notice and sighed quietly in resignation.

"Mister Andretti," Phoss called out to Johnny. "As you can see, by special directive from the Office of the Consuls of the UER, you have now been augmented from the Reserves into the Space Force Marines Regulars at the rank of Colonel. Congratulations on your promotion and augmentation. I have made arrangements for you to undergo a one-on-one bulldog session of actual Marine training to legitimize your commission in the Corps. Chief Lowdon and Gunny Zheng will handle your training."

"There is one, more pleasant thing," Phoss pressed a button again and their communicators chimed. "Congratulation Bill. We'll do this formally in a few days."

Johnny read the message and laughed out loud. "Trading your eagle for a star. Makes you a Commodore? Well, you'll always be Skipper to me. Congratulations on the promotion."

Farragut smiled, always a frightening thing. "Now, I can court martial your insubordinate ass and it will stick like white on rice."

Johnny's head was spinning with all the promotions and inductions. At the center of the whirlwind in his mind he held fast to one thought. *They bought all of it. If the Thalyrians do too, the con is on. Time to make this real in ways his three stooges and dos amigos might not fully appreciate.*

28. Union Shop

Two days later it was Johnny who was smiling. Even though he was back in Farragut's office facing his wrath.

"What the Hell is this?" Farragut snarled, brusquely shoving a message flimsy across his desk toward Johnny.

Johnny glanced at the message without picking it up. He knew what it said.

"Aren't you going to congratulate me Skipper? You're looking at the new President of the Space Plumbers Union, and the Shop Steward for SPU Local 001."[14]

"I don't give a rat's rear about meaningless titles. What's this about Arnold and Hess?" Both were standing silently at attention behind Johnny. Gunnery Sergeant Zheng stood off to one side. Also, at attention.

The two young men paled slightly in the face of Farragut's obvious fury.

"Sir, we …," Arnold began.

---

[14] See BF-B-097 ORIGIN OF THE SPACE PLUMBERS UNION

BF-B-098 THE MAKING OF THE SPACE PLUMBERS UNION

BF-B-099 THE NIGHT THE UNION WAS BOUGHT Black File All Access Required.

Johnny held up one hand toward the two, cautioning them to silence.

"The SPU has bought out the remainder of the enlistments of these two Marines, enrolled them as members of SPU Local 001, and hired them as apprentice fluid mechanics."

"Gunny Zheng, did you know about this? Aren't you their Platoon Sergeant?"

"Yes Sir, I am their Platoon Sergeant. The first I heard of this was less than an hour ago."

"Skipper, if I may," Johnny spoke up, "in fairness to Zheng, and to you, this really all came together in just the last twenty-four hours. I made this offer to the boys early this morning, although I already had everything set to drop."

"You expect me to believe you bought out their enlistments before you even talked with them?"

Johnny shrugged. "It was a calculated risk."

Farragut's jaw clenched for a brief moment. Johnny could see the moment when Farragut moved on. His jaw unclenched. "What happens now?"

"These two," Johnny nodded toward Arnold and Hess, "will be processed out of the Corps over the next ten days. Their clearances remain intact. They will need to relocate to civilian quarters here on Odyssey. Oh, and I will need a meeting hall for the Union which will include an office befitting my role as the Union President."

"Befitting your role?" Farragut sputtered. "Marines, you're dismissed." Zheng, Hess, and Arnold snapped to attention and marched out of the room.

After the door closed Farragut spoke. "I ask again. What happens now?"

Johnny smiled, a genuinely warm grin. "According to Phoss, everything." *We'll keep the pipes flowing and the secrets buried—just not always in the order Command expected.*

Epilogue

Figure 6 Escape

Johnny rolled his shoulders to work out the residual pain from his training with Gunny Zheng. With an impatient jab of his finger, he approved the report in front of him and registered the number of reports still in his queue. As he watched, it went up by three. He sighed. *Paperwork will kill me before any hitter can.*

He knew he had no right to complain. Everything was going according to plan. The Space Plumbers Union was responsible for a significant improvement in all the work being done in space, and it was a perfect cover for their entire spy agency.

His communicator pinged. It was Farragut. *Thank God.* He thought, then paused. *How screwed is my universe where a call from Farragut is a welcome relief.*

"Skipper?" he answered the comm.

"Andretti, why are you telling me about an AWOL fluids tech?"

"Rao came on my radar while looking into Ham. He was the hub for a water theft racket. I wanted to co-opt him, or take him off the board."

"Did either happen?"

"No Skipper. I gave him a squeeze and he bolted. Kid was a poser anyway."

"Hiding on the Odyssey?"

"Looks like he jumped ship." Johnny tapped some keys and a short report popped up on Farragut's screen. Johnny narrated, "About ten minutes before things went pear shaped for me in Blister 61 someone matching his description caught a freighter headed Earth-ward. Used a forged identity. I followed up and found some scraps in his trash that fit with faking cards."

"He deserted?"

"Looks like. If my friends in the Longshoreman Union come through. I'll see when and where he landed and walked off. Probably have him in hand in twenty-four."

"A pointless distraction. Move on."

Johnny shrugged. "You're the boss." *More of a distraction than you know,* he thought.

"Put out a BOLO on him. If the cops ever pick him up, they'll drag his deserter ass right back to us."

"You got it Skipper." *No BOLO will ever match Rao's face to whatever was left of him after he was sucked into space through a two-inch wide hull breach.* Farragut continued staring at him, not breaking the connection. "Something else bothering you today, Skipper?"

"Remember the other day when you were jaw jacking about how well things are going?"

"Sure." Johnny agreed with a smile. "You told me that being happy about how smoothly things were going was a sure way to jinx it?"

"The Consortium notified us that two of their ice haulers have fallen off the grid. Implement Operation Blackout right away."

"It's not fully baked yet. Our asset is close to AguaLibre, but still outside. Slipping in a backstopped story that Sanctifiers are to blame will be a challenge."

"I told you not to jinx it." The call ended.

Johnny shook his head, anger, frustration, and disbelief in three equal and violent factions doing battle in his head. Finally, he surrendered, "I jinxed it."

A single line cut across his screen, "EYES ONLY FLASH: Station 77B3 under attack."

If bad things come in threes, I don't wanna know what's next. But wherever water was bleeding out into the void, somebody was about to need a plumber.

His desk communicator lit up. *How much worse can this day get?*

"Andretti here," he answered. When the face he was seeing registered with his brain he felt a bucket of ice water poured down his back.

"Johnny Alliata. So good to *catch up with you.* I've got a complaint about your plumbing work in Vegas. Time to pay the piper, Johnny," Tony Gambino, the consigliere of the Gambino crime family smiled coldly at him through the video link.

And there's three.

BLACK FILES

Some records are not archived.
Some events are not reported.
Some systems do not fail the way they are supposed to.

The official record reflects what can be explained, verified, and contained. It does not reflect what operators see when systems behave outside their design limits.

Black Files exist to capture those discrepancies.

They are not complete. They are not always consistent. They are not intended for public circulation.

Each file represents a point where:

- a system behaved incorrectly
- a decision was made off the record
- an outcome could not be reconciled with the explanation provided

Individually, they can be dismissed. Taken together, they suggest a pattern.

Access to these materials is restricted.

Interpretation is left to the reader.

Proceed accordingly.

UNION ACCESS BRIEF
File: BF-U-006
Title: *Blood and Ice*
Access Level: Union
Function: Background / Personnel Origin Event

Summary

This file documents the events that made Johnny Alliata into "The Plumber" long before Odyssey, the war, or the name carried weight beyond South Philly.

The immediate trigger was his father's death.

What followed was not grief alone, but a method.

Note

This account records the point at which Johnny stops being a gifted apprentice with sharp eyes
and becomes something far more dangerous: a man who learns to find leaks in systems made of people.

Blood and Ice

A Plumbing Space™ Black File

By

Thomas K Sheppard

South Philly smelled like burnt oil, boiled rats, and betrayal. Pietro Giovanni 'Johnny' Alliata wiped his hands on the legs of his jumpsuit, smearing rust and grit across the navy blue. He glanced at his watch. *One in the morning. Gonna get in trouble falling asleep in school again,* Johnny thought. It wouldn't be the first time.

His father, Giuseppe, was still inside the drydock utility vault, arguing with a supervisor about the access valve. Johnny had handled the soldering like a pro, smooth as copper in water. Officially, he was a fifteen-year-old apprentice plumber in Philadelphia Local 317. Unofficially, he was already better than half the guys drawing journeyman pay.

He and Pop, or Gus as his coworkers called Giuseppe, had been working since 4 that afternoon fixing busted water mains beneath a condemned warehouse; one of those waterfront jobs where everything was damp, and nothing was clean. The kind of place where the mob buried cash and the cops dug up problems and a kid like Johnny learned to keep his mouth shut and his eyes open.

He heard the sirens before he saw the lights.

Three blacked-out cruisers rolled into the yard, unmarked but unmistakable. Johnny ducked into the crawlspace, heart hammering. From his vantage point, he saw the officers pour out, vests on, weapons drawn. A raid. Fast. Surgical. Like they knew exactly where to go.

Two arrests. One shootout. One dead.

Giuseppe came out zipped in a black bag.

The funeral was small. Union brothers, mostly. A priest with no homily. A mother too angry to cry.

So much for college, Johnny thought. Jumping a year of school and having a solid GPA wouldn't keep a roof over their heads. He sat in silence, hands folded, a half-burned apprentice card in his back pocket.

The cops didn't call it murder. The report listed it as "accidental discharge during a lawful action." But everyone knew the cops had raided the wrong place—or the right place, with the wrong man inside.

Rumors spread like mold in the pipes. There was a rat. Someone feeding the feds. Someone close.

This rat had just stolen bread off his mother's plate and joy from her eyes. Johnny decided he'd find him.

He started with what he knew—flow. Water. Systems. Leaks. Pressure.

"Every system leaks," his father had said once. "You just gotta know where to feel for heat."

Johnny applied the same logic to people. He watched who stopped showing up at the docks. Who suddenly had new clothes, new shoes. Who didn't meet your eyes in the break room.

Below average height, average build, for a man; at 15 he'd put on all the height he was getting in this life. He wasn't a bone breaker, but long hours of turning wrenches and lifting pipes made him hard and strong. His mind, behind glinting dark eyes, was sharper than any mugger's knife. He could see patterns where others only saw dust.

He kept a notebook in the liner of his tool bag; routes, timings, faces. His evenings were spent in the corners of bars or shadowing runners, ducking through side alleys. The city's veins were mapped in his head like blueprints. And the pressure points? They always revealed themselves.

The cops didn't want help.

Detective Marshal, the one working his father's case, brushed him off. But Johnny kept showing up. Offering questions instead of answers. Marshal saw the hunger and dropped crumbs.

"You want to catch a killer, Alliata? Learn to think like one."

So, Johnny read. Doyle. Hammett. The classics. He learned how real detectives worked—how they broke alibis, dissected motives, watched for the tells. It wasn't fiction to him. It was a trade. Plumbing for truth.

His suspect list narrowed fast.

Vic Santos. Ex-foreman. Smart. Liked to talk union politics but never stayed for drinks. Disappeared right after the raid. Showed back up with a gold watch and no tools.

One night, Johnny tailed him. Santos didn't go to work. He went to a dead-end block near 10th Street, met with a man in a sedan, and handed off a folder. Johnny noted the plates. The sedan belonged to a narcotics task force.

Vic was a CI. Confidential Informant. A rat.

Vic's apartment was three flights up in a rotting walkup. No one gave a second look at the grimy-faced guy in plumber's togs with a toolbox in hand. Another clogged sink pipe or stopped toilet to fix. Someone else's problem.

Johnny picked the lock with a plumber's probe and slipped inside. The heat inside was thick, summer sweat and old beer. He moved fast. Behind the toilet tank, taped to the ceramic, he found a plastic bag.

Inside: burner phone, payout receipts, an envelope of hundred dollar bills, printed maps with marked locations, and a small notebook in Vic's handwriting. Marks on the map included the one where Giuseppe had died.

He heard the door latch click.

Vic stepped inside, stopped cold. Johnny didn't flinch.

"You're Gus' kid."

"And you're the leak."

Vic chuckled, slow and venomous, closing the door tight behind him. "Your old man got nosy. Wasn't supposed to be there."

"You killed him."

"Nah. The cops did. I just lit the fuse."

Johnny didn't remember picking up the cheater bar, and Vic didn't see it coming in the semidarkness. The first swing was instinct, the blow caught Vic on the jaw, dropping him in his tracks. The second was rage, on the top of his head. The third... the third was quiet. Blood soaked into the old, stained, area rug like water from a split valve.

Johnny found the bleach, spraying it everywhere. He rolled the body in the rug and let adrenaline do the heavy lifting; carrying the body down the stairs and into the trunk of Vic's car.

A bit of cash from Vic's stash made the night watchman on the construction site go blind and deaf while the boy used a backhoe to dig the foundation hole eight feet deeper and used the backhoe to push Vic and his car into the hole. He tamped down the dirt on top and parked the equipment where he had found it.

By dawn, the foundation crew poured three feet of concrete into the hole; giving Vic a permanent change of address, beneath a new South Philly apartment complex.

They grabbed him the next day. Black SUV. No questions.

Tony Capaldi was short, going bald, and skirting the edge of being morbidly obese. Johnny knew him by reputation and face. His Pops made sure of that, and made sure the two never met. Tony was the local Capo. He sat behind a butcher block table in a cold storage room beneath a butcher shop, staring at Johnny with disbelief writ large on his florid face.

Two soldiers stood flanking Johnny.. Pillars of bone and muscle. *Probably without half a brain between them,* Johnny thought.

"You kill one of mine, kid?"

"Maybe. Who you askin' about?"

The Capo laughed. "Look at this kid. Asking which body, like he drops 'em all the time." The soldiers smiled and chuckled dutifully. Tony nodded and one backhanded Johnny hard across the side of his head, making his ears ring.

"You kill Vic Santos, you little wiseass?"

"Damn right I did," Johnny snarled. "He was a rat, a leaky pipe. Got my Pops killed."

Tony leaned back and studied Johnny. "Well, ain't you full of piss and vinegar? You know, back in the day, the name Alliata meant something. Sicilian royalty."

Johnny glared. "Still does. Translates to 'gets it done when others can't.' Soldiers, hustlers, corner-boys, and bent cops have been beatin' the streets for weeks hunting a rat; trying to plug your leak. I'm Johnny Alliata, the plumber who finds leaks and ends 'em."

One of the soldiers cocked his arm for another slap, but a slight shake of the head from Tony stopped it.

"Why you sayin' Vic was a rat?"

Johnny nodded toward the bag they had pulled out of his coat when they brought him in. "It's all in there."

A soldier handed the bag to Tony, who opened it and spread the contents across the butcher block. He thumbed through the receipts, the maps, the burner phone. He lingered over a small notebook written in Vic's choppy hand, and another in Johnny's tight writing. Silent.

"Where'd you find this?"

Johnny told him about the break-in, the search, and confrontation with Vic.

"The body?"

"You really wanna know?" Johnny challenged.

Tony sat silent again, studying Johnny.

"This blows back on me…" Tony started to threaten.

"How can it?" Johnny interrupted. "You know exactly two things about Vic Santo. He was a leaky sewer pipe and now he isn't."

"You forgot the third thing I know, wiseass."

"What's that?"

"I know you killed him."

"You've only got my word on that."

"You a man of your word?"

"I am," Johnny shot back without hesitation.

A long silence. In Tony's eyes, Johnny saw the coins shift, until the scale tipped.

Then: "Johnny 'the Plumber' Alliata, all over this town we got pipes that break. Deals that leak. Men who talk. You think you can handle more of these sorts of plumbing jobs?"

Johnny sat up straight. "Pops taught me plumbing, and the street. I'll find and fix your leaks."

"I believe you. Keep your eyes open, your mouth shut, and your hands clean, you'll eat better than most."

Johnny nodded once.

Tony nodded to one of the soldiers, "Go upstairs and take a dime from petty cash. Give it to the plumber on his way out."

His mother never asked where the ten grand to pay the rent and groceries came from, and Johnny never offered. His was that sort of family.

Six months later, he was back under the docks, tightening fittings with a pipe wrench. The phone in his pocket vibrated twice, then stopped. He checked the number and dialed a different one.

"You good for an urgent plumbing job in South Jersey? Bosses say they got a leak they can't find. Needs a quiet fix."

Johnny wiped his hands on an old rag and slipped the wrench into his toolbox.

"Yeah," he said. "I'll fix it."

And he did.

Every time.

FILE NOTE
File: BF-U-006
Access Level: Union
The immediate issue was the death of Johnny's father and the identification of the man responsible.

The larger issue was what Johnny would become once he proved he could find a leak, close it, and live with the result.

He proved it.

That is what matters here.

Outcome

- Responsible leak: identified
- Personal threshold: crossed
- Johnny's role: established

This is the point at which Johnny Alliata stops being merely a plumber by trade and begins becoming The Plumber by reputation.

Continue in the Archive

If you liked the grime, the pressure, and the kind of problems you cannot solve with a gun, there is a deeper layer of **Plumbing Space™** waiting.

Not everything fits in the books.

Most of it never makes the official record.

The file included in this volume is only one recovered record from the **Union Access** archive.

Additional Union Access Black Files, dossiers, world intel, and early access materials are available through the official Plumbing Space archive.

Inside the Archive:

- **Black Files:** Off-record stories that show what really happened
- **Character Dossiers:** The motives, histories, and fractures the crew does not share
- **World Intel:** Timelines, systems, and the trade that makes water worth killing for
- **Advance Access:** Early entry into upcoming books and releases

Access the Archive: www.AccessPlumbingSpace.com

About the Author

Tom Sheppard is a program manager in the U.S. financial services industry by day and a bestselling author by night.

He has authored more than 50 titles across business and fiction, with several more in progress.

Follow Tom:
https://www.facebook.com/AuthorTomSheppard/

Also by Tom Sheppard

The Masterless Sword: Book 1 – Origins

Michael Galliger is a brilliant scientist. Tasked with creating an army to defend his country, but who can wield such a terrible weapon and not be consumed by it?

The Masterless Sword: Book 2 – Rise of the Master Mage

Science becomes magic as civilization collapses and nanotechnology, bioengineering and genetic engineering combine to create servants who will carve out their own destinies in the new world amid the ruins of the old.

The Masterless Sword: Book 3 –Queen of the Wildwood

Human civilization has collapsed.
Who will control the creatures of the wildwood? The fate of humanity hinges on the the Queen of the Wildwood.

Coming Soon

Plumbing Space Book 2: Pressure Lines

The UER prepares for open conflict with the Sanctifiers while Johnny and the Space Plumbers' Union quietly redirect the flow of money, water, and weapons.

Plumbing Space Book 3: Backflow

As the Sanctifier fleet advances, Johnny and the Union become the last line of defense between Earth and exploitation.

www.ingramcontent.com/pod-product-compliance
Lightning Source LLC
LaVergne TN
LVHW091053080826
845145LV00002B/731

* 9 7 8 1 9 6 7 5 4 8 0 9 5 *